RUMPOLE AND THE
PENGE BUNGALOW MURDERS

Old men forget and all shall be forgot
Yet I'll remember with advantages
what feats I did that day

Rumpole took the liberty of altering Shakespeare a little when he offered the meeing at his Chambers a choice quotation from *Henry V*. It reflected what he was thinking: that he should commit to paper his memories of the Penge Bungalow affair before the details of such a case were to become lost in the mists of time.

Horace Rumpole had been a novice when the murders at Penge first hit the headlines: two war heroes, bomber pilots, apparently shot dead after a reunion dinner by the son of one of them, Simon Jerold.

Young he might have been, but in those days Simon Jerold was facing the ultimate punishment. There seemed little hope, since the evidence against him was so incriminating. But something about it bothered Rumpole, and when the time came for him to seize the initiative, he did it triumphantly—like King Harry himself.

First published 2004
by
Viking

Will no one tell me what she sings?—
Perhaps the plaintive numbers flow
For old, unhappy, far-off things,
And battles long ago:

Wordsworth, 'The Solitary Reaper'

1

'Claude Erskine-Brown told my pupil she had extraordinarily nice legs.'

'What're her legs like, then? Rather gnarled tree trunks, are they?'

'Don't be ridiculous, Rumpole! Lala Ingolsby is a very good-looking girl.'

'With a name like Lala Ingolsby I should have thought she wouldn't mind having her legs complimented.'

'She wouldn't mind! That's what you all say, don't you, Rumpole? Just like a man! Anyway, I have reported Erskine-Brown's conduct to the Chair of the Society of Women Barristers.'

The speaker was Mizz Liz Probert, my one-time pupil and in many ways a helpful and hard-working barrister, when she was not determined to throw the book at Claude Erskine-Brown. He was being tried *in absentia*, having left early to catch about twenty-four hours of the Ring Cycle at Covent Garden.

'Through the Chair!' Luci Gribble, our chambers Director of Marketing and Administration, spoke urgently to Soapy Sam Ballard, our Head of Chambers.

He looked both pained and startled, as though this 'Through the Chair' form of address involved some kind of physical attack and penetration.

'Through the Chair!' Luci (who spelled her name with an inexplicable 'i') repeated. 'It will be no good at all for our chambers' image if we get a reputation in the Society of Women Barristers for

1

acts of sexual harassment.'

It's rare indeed that I am present at chambers meetings, held under the chairmanship of Soapy Sam Ballard and dealing often with such vital matters as the expenditure on instant coffee in the clerk's room or the importance of leaving a signed bit of paper on the library shelves when borrowing a book. But these were the dog days in the cold, wet and bleak start of the year, the criminals of England seemed to have all gone off for a winter break to Marbella or the Seychelles, and I had wandered into Ballard's room as an alternative to yet another struggle with the crossword puzzle.

'I suppose I must have words with Erskine-Brown on the subject.' Soapy Sam sounded despondent, as though he were being asked to take immediate action about the condition of the downstairs lavatory in Equity Court.

'You could tell Miss Ingolsby that if nothing worse happens to her, in her life in the law, she'll have been remarkably lucky. Come to think of it, at about her age I was doing the Penge Bungalow Murders, alone and without a leader.'

As I said this, the chambers meeting and all its concerns seemed to fade away. For a moment I was back long ago. I remembered myself sitting in an interview room under the Old Bailey, looking into the terrified eyes of a young man who had realized that the great engine of the criminal law was intent on driving him towards a grim execution shed and ceremoniously breaking his neck.

Then Luci Gribble startled me with an extraordinary question. 'What on earth,' she asked, without a note of shame in her voice, 'were the Penge Bungalow Murders?'

2

I was, I have to confess, shaken by such ignorance of one of the most remarkable trials of the post-war years; but in all fairness I had to concede that Luci Gribble was a lay person with no legal training. The story would take too long if I went into it myself and so I appointed Liz Probert to act for me.

'You tell her, Liz.'

'I'm not sure . . .' For the first time in the meeting, the politically correct Mizz Probert was caught off her guard. 'I'm not sure I ever knew the facts,' she astounded me by admitting. 'Before my time, of course.'

'Ballard?' I appealed to our so-called Head of Chambers.

'I'm not sure I ever knew what went on in the Penge bungalows either,' he said, as though one of my greatest legal triumphs were something that just slips the mind, like where you put the bus ticket. 'I've heard you speak of it, Rumpole, of course, on many occasions. *You* clearly remember it.'

'Old men forget,' I gave the meeting a well-deserved thought from *Henry V*, 'and all shall be forgot. Yet I'll remember with advantages what feats I did that day.'

Of course, I altered the quotation a little to suit my purpose. But it was then that I realized it was high time I added the full story of the Penge Bungalow affair to my memoirs. So much of history is being lost. Young people nowadays are vague as to the identity of Hitler and Churchill, and although the murders at Penge were once headline material, the details of that remarkable case may have become lost in the mists of time.

3

We're looking back, down the long corridor of history, to the early 1950s. The war had been over for several years, but it still seemed part of our lives. Films featured life and death in the skies during the Battle of Britain, and heroes or heroines of the Resistance. It was a period when those who had enjoyed an unheroic war continued to feel pangs of guilt, and we all congratulated ourselves on having survived the Blitz, bread rationing, the Labour chancellor telling us all to 'tighten our belts' and clothes on coupons.

It was, in many ways, an age of obedience when the government, the royal family and judges were treated with what was sometimes ill-deserved respect. It was also the time when the only sentence available for murder was death.

My own war had been unheroic. I had spent some years in the RAF ground staff (where I was well known as 'Grounded Rumpole') and, when hostilities ended, I had taken a law degree at Keble College, Oxford. As learning law in those days entailed an intimate knowledge of the Roman rules for freeing a slave and the rights of 'turfage' over common land (scraps of information which I have never found of the slightest use in the Uxbridge Magistrates' Court) and as I never at Keble experienced the excitement of rising on my then young hind legs to address a jury, I turned in a fairly honourable third-class degree. It has always been my view that knowing too much law is not only no help but also a considerable handicap to the courtroom advocate. Juries, on the whole, have little interest in freeing slaves or the Roman law governing the ownership of chariots.

My tutor at Keble had been Septimus Porter. I had loved his shy and nervous, but sometimes unexpectedly liberated, daughter dearly. In fact we were engaged to be married, but this engagement had to be broken off because of Ivy Porter's early death during the cold winter and fuel shortages after the war. Septimus Porter found me a place in the chambers of C. H. Wystan, QC, the father of that Hilda Wystan who was to become known to me, during a long life of argument and dispute both in and away from the courtroom, as She Who Must Be Obeyed.

Wystan's importance, therefore, both in the events surrounding the Penge Bungalow affair and in my future career and life, cannot be exaggerated.

2

The appearance of C. H. Wystan always made me think of some harmless crustacean, perhaps a lobster who had been snatched from a peaceful existence at the bottom of the sea and plunged into boiling water. His face and bald head were of a uniform pink, his mouth was turned down as though in sudden shock and his small beady eyes gave him a look of pained surprise. When he spoke he often moved his arms in the slow, disconnected way that lobsters have. But I have no wish to be overly critical of my future father-in-law. It was not after all his fault that he had, to my eye at least, the appearance of something that might be cooled down and served up with a hard-boiled egg and a dab of mayonnaise.

C. H. Wystan was in no way a bad man. In fact he treated me, during my early years as a white wig, with a sort of remote and distant kindness. The trouble was that he regarded the whole business of being a barrister, and following in what he called 'the fine traditions and great fellowship of the bar' (such rules as 'We don't shake hands' or 'We don't lunch with our instructing solicitor'), as more important than the Bill of Rights or the presumption of innocence. Like Soapy Sam Ballard, our present Head of Chambers, the niceties and formalities of life in the law were to him more precious than justice. Law courts were places where honourable men (there were, as yet, no female barristers in Equity Court), dressed in wigs, gowns and appropriately dark trousers, lived up to their finest traditions. He found the cases in which we dabbled, the adulterous, fraudulent or violent acts alleged against our clients, the indecencies or even the murders they might have committed, of less interest than the correct behaviour of the barristers and judges sent to try them. He dined frequently in his Inn and was always available to take a bishop or a senior politician in to dinner on his arm. Judges found his behaviour in court impeccable, but his score of victories was low. All the same, he was considered so trustworthy that the Lord Chancellor felt able to give him a silk gown, so that he now proudly bore the letters QC (Queer Customer, I'm inclined to call them) after his name. Solicitors thought of him as 'a safe pair of hands'.

The hands I was put into when I first arrived at number 4 Equity Court were not so much safe as inactive. 'We've fixed up a pupillage for you with T. C. Rowley,' Wystan said. 'You'll find him an agreeable pupil master. He's very well liked in chambers, where he's affectionately known as "Uncle Tom". It would be wrong to describe him as a *busy* practitioner, but he'll have plenty of time to iron out problems and give you the benefit of his long experience.'

After introducing me to the clerk's room and to one or two important-looking barristers, who were apparently too busy to iron out the problems of a white wig, he showed me into T. C. Rowley's room, where I sat expectantly at a small table in the corner to await events.

Events, as such, were extremely slow in arriving, as indeed was T. C. Rowley himself. 'We're expecting Uncle Tom in before the end of the month,' was the constant answer in the clerk's room when I asked if he was likely to drop in to chambers. So I sat alone and got to know our room by heart, the few legal textbooks and law reports, the reproduction of *The Stag at Bay* over the fireplace, the tin box which no doubt contained Uncle Tom's apparently little-used wig, the bottom drawer of the desk, which concealed a few back numbers of *Naturist* magazine, and, most puzzling of all, a golf club in the umbrella stand.

Each morning I stared out of the window and watched busy barristers, chattering importantly, setting out for court with their junior clerks carrying briefs or pushing trolleyloads of books. Each evening I stayed until the lamplighter, with a flaming rod, lit the gas lamps in Equity Court. When it became apparent that I was not going to have many problems to iron out if I remained closeted in Uncle Tom's quarters, I began to haunt the clerk's room, which I rightly guessed to be the centre of chambers activity, much in the way that dogs sniff around kitchen floors in the faint hope of picking up a few scraps.

Albert Handyside, then our head clerk, was a large, slow-moving man whose pockets were overflowing with cause lists, notes of fees, messages from solicitors and packets of small cigars. His apparently gloomy outlook on life concealed a deep inner hilarity. If, by some joke of fate, C. H. Wystan found himself briefed in two different cases at the same time, Albert would shake with silent mirth but then, after a tactful visit to the Old Bailey list office, solve the problem by persuading a judge to sit later or a prosecutor to agree to prolong his final speech. Most of his business was conducted with solicitors' clerks in Pommeroy's Wine Bar, where they swapped stories and pints of Guinness. There he persuaded them, or so I hoped, to sample, perhaps in a little matter of assault and affray at East Ham Quarter Sessions, the talents of a white wig new to chambers by the name of Horace Rumpole.

I have to say I did my very best to cultivate the friendship of Albert Handyside, who I knew would be of far more use to me than the elusive Uncle Tom, or even C. H. Wystan himself. I spent time, and money I could ill afford, in Pommeroy's seeing that Albert's glass of Guinness was continually refilled. My attentions were rewarded. He sent me off to fix a date for trial at London Sessions. I did this, after an evening of anxious rehearsal, apparently to everyone's satisfaction.

It was when I came back from this courtroom triumph that I heard, as I approached my usually lonely room, the sound of a golf club striking a ball. I opened the door to see a tall, even a gangling, grey-haired man smiling with delight as a golf ball sailed into a wastepaper basket. 'Hello, young fellow,' he greeted me. 'I'm Uncle Tom and you're my pupil.'

I had to admit that this was indeed the truth of the matter.

'I was waiting for you to come in,' he said. 'In fact I wondered where the hell you'd got to. Having a lie-in, were you—after a heavy night?'

'Not really. I was making an application at London Sessions.'

'An application! At your stage?' Uncle Tom gave a small whistle of admiration as he put his golf balls back in the oval black and gold box which was built to contain a wig. 'Bit of a fast mover, aren't you, Rumbelow?'

'The name,' I told him, 'is Rumpole.'

'I hope you weren't waiting for me to come with you. Show you the ropes. You managed it on your own?'

'I managed it,' I told him, 'entirely on my own.'

'Good for you, then. I'll tell Wystan that I've got a most promising pupil.'

In those far-off days young barristers had to pay £100 to be 'taught' by their pupil masters. Uncle Tom had it from a legacy my old father received from my great-aunt. I didn't begrudge him this money, although he told me it came in very useful in settling his golf club subscription at a time when the secretary had given him 'a couple of old-fashioned looks'. He wasn't entirely without work: he had two long-running divorce cases and an extremely slow-moving post office fraud in which he had occasional conferences with a solicitor called 'Nobby' Noakes, who chatted to Uncle Tom about his golf handicap, much to the boredom of their client. In time we came to an unspoken agreement. Uncle Tom visited the room even less often and I was in sole possession of his desk as my practice didn't exactly flower but put out a few tender and tentative shoots.

When I look back on that Rumpole, the inexperienced and more or less unlearned friend who could suffer nervous attacks, a dry mouth, sweaty hands and a strong temptation to run out of the building before entering the humblest magistrates' court to do the simplest careless driving, I can scarcely recognize him. Indeed I'm not at all sure that I would like him, at least not

11

enough to spend a whole book with him, were it not for the fact that he gave me some hints, at least, of the Rumpole to come.

For instance, one evening when I was having a drink with Albert in Pommeroy's, I said I felt in the mood for a glass of red wine. 'You won't get any of your vintage claret here,' Albert said, and I can remember asking if it were more 'your non-vintage Château Thames Embankment'. This produced a loud rumble of laughter from Albert Handyside and a name for a wine which seems to have survived for about half a century, and when old Vernon Pommeroy was succeeded by his son Jack the change caused no perceptible improvement in the wine. It was also at Pommeroy's that Albert offered me one of his small cigars, introducing me to a source of comfort and relaxation when the insolence of office and the law's delays had become almost too much to bear.

So, by regular attendance at chambers and in Pommeroy's Wine Bar, I had managed to win a reasonable number of taking and driving aways, actual bodily harms and minor indecencies round a number of fairly unsympathetic courts. I could see myself, in the years to come, as the moderately successful, middle-of-the-road type of advocate of whom we had quite a few in our chambers.

And then, as I say, the double murder in the Penge bungalows hit the headlines and changed my life.

I had, for many years, been aware of Penge. My father, the Reverend Wilfred Rumpole, had charge of a church (St Botolph's Without) in the neighbouring suburb of Croydon. My old father was not entirely happy in his work. He had serious doubts, he once told me, about most of the Thirty-Nine Articles; but his training had not equipped him for any other job, so he was compelled to soldier on at St Botolph's.

In my early years I seem to have spent more time in a bleak boarding school on the Norfolk coast or at Keble College than I did in the south London suburbs. When I got a place in C. H. Wystan's chambers I made a determined bid for independence and took a room in the house of a Mrs Matilda Ruben, who not only let out bedsits but owned a small shop for the sale of trusses and other surgical appliances, including what, in those far-off days, we used to call 'rubber johnnies', in a street just off Southampton Row. This was in walking distance of the Temple. There were, I promise you, briefless days when I had to become a walker in order to save on bus fares.

I had, however, a clear memory of Penge, a small suburb beside the island of parkland surrounding the old Crystal Palace, now burnt down, where I used to go on walks with my father and listen to his serious doubts on the subjects of God's toleration of evil and original sin. I even remembered the street of bungalows which had sprung up in the 1930s to accommodate the growing population of the families of bank clerks, department store managers and commercial travellers who looked on Crystal Palace Park as their particular and privileged glimpse of the countryside.

The facts of the double murder in the bungalows emerged from the newspapers which I read, rather as a young man hitchhiking through Somerset might read of a voyage of discovery in darkest Africa, never dreaming that I would come any nearer to the case than the full story in what we then called the 'News of the Screws'.

Denis, always known as 'Jerry', Jerold was a clerk at the National Provincial Bank when he got married to Yvonne and moved into their bungalow, number 3 Paxton Street. There they had their only child, Simon. When the war started, Jerry joined the RAF and soon became a bomber pilot. His life was less exciting when peace returned him to the bank, but his bungalow was filled with relics of the war: photographs of himself scrambling into his bomber, drinking and laughing with his fellow officers, together with his carefully preserved uniform, the silk scarf always tied at his throat when on a mission, fragments of destroyed enemy aircraft and a Luger pistol taken from the body of a dead enemy officer. Also prominent in the photographs was Charlie ('Tail-End' Charlie) Weston, who lived at number 7 Paxton Street. He joined up with Jerry and, by a series of lucky chances, was Jerry's rear gunner. After the war, Charlie Weston returned to his bungalow and his job at the Happy Home Mortgage and Insurance Company.

Both Jerry and Charlie survived the war, but Yvonne, Jerry's wife and Simon's mother, was

14

killed by a buzz bomb when she was out shopping just north of Oxford Street in the closing stages of the war.

After his wife's death, according to the *News of the World*, Jerry moved in, from time to time, a series of girlfriends, but none of them lasted long and for considerable periods father and son were living alone in the bungalow.

On the night of the murders Jerry and Charlie had been at a reunion dinner of members of the old squadron living in and around Croydon. Some they had known well, some were almost strangers. After the dinner and seeing Judy Garland at the London Palladium, singing and more than a little drunk, they came back to Jerry's bungalow, where they woke up Simon and the party continued. During the course of it, according to the evidence given at a preliminary hearing before the Penge magistrates, a quarrel sprang up between father and son and young Simon was seen to pick up the German pistol and threaten his father and other members of the party. At that point he was quite easily disarmed by one of the RAF companions, after which he shut himself in his room.

The party continued for a while, but in the morning young Simon rang the police to say that he had found his father dead, shot through the heart. 'Tail-End' Charlie was later found dead in his bungalow. Apparently he'd been shot when answering the door to some late-night caller. Both men were killed by German bullets. The pistol and magazine with two of its bullets fired were found in the dustbin outside the Jerolds' back door.

Jerry's son was arrested and charged with a double murder. As though he weren't in enough trouble already, he asked to see the only solicitor he'd ever heard of. This was a Penge local who had done a number of civil cases with my Head of Chambers, for whom the solicitor had a surprisingly high regard.

So Simon Jerold, being just over twenty-one, was old enough for national service and old enough to be hanged. And it was on C. H. Wystan that his life depended.

4

There is no point in writing your memoirs unless you're prepared to tell the truth, and I have to confess to a number of occasions when I have felt stirred by an often hopeless passion and believed myself deeply in love. At Keble I had loved my fiancÈe, Ivy Porter, who was carried off in the cold snap after the war. When I was a member of the ground staff I was helplessly smitten by an alluring WAAF named Bobby O'Keefe, with whom I enjoyed a brief but ecstatic love affair until she was wooed from me by the then heroic charm of a certain pilot officer, Sam 'Three Fingers' Dougherty, who flew Spitfires and had apparently lost one of his fingers in action. I felt hidden longings, many years later, for a Kathy Trelawny, a beautiful if somewhat spaced-out member of the 'alternative society' who, ignoring my advice to stay silent at her trial, talked her way into Holloway Prison, where I had to say goodbye to her.

In the early 1950s, when peace and some degree of prosperity were celebrated by the Festival of Britain, the Dome of Discovery, the Guinness Clock and other tributes to our national way of life, including the Penge Bungalow Murders, I felt my existence enriched by a Miss Daisy Sampson. She was an outdoor clerk in the firm of Mickelthwaite and Nutwell, which was, by then, briefing me in small cases in the magistrates' courts. She was blonde, cheerful and uninhibited, a girl with a ready smile, slightly protruding front teeth outlined with bright red lipstick and a way with fairly basic jokes, such as 'I'm always going to give you my briefs, Mr Rumpole,' which I found, in those far-off years, both provocative and witty.

So we shared morning coffee and pub lunches round the Uxbridge Magistrates', Old Street, Bow Street and the Horseferry Road. We spoke disrespectfully of our clients, the chairmen of the benches and the magistrates' clerks, and were able, more often than not, to pull off some sort of victory. Our relationship had so far advanced that, when I saw a dance for junior members of the bar and their guests announced in the Inner Temple Hall, I decided in a moment of reckless extravagance on the hire of a dinner jacket and tickets, supper included, for self and Daisy Sampson.

> We were waltzin' together to a dreamy melody
> When they called out 'Change partners'
> And you waltzed away from me.

Although I was slowly gaining some experience as a barrister, I had far less experience as a dancer. Miss Daisy Sampson was so unfailingly cheerful and tolerant, however, that I was able to stroll round the dance floor, keeping my arm around her waist and my feet out of her way, and I imagined myself entirely happy in the early part of that evening.

And then, even as we danced, I heard a high commanding voice, the bray of an Eton accent, and turned to recognize Reginald 'Reggie' Proudfoot, who had been the prosecutor in some of our cases.

'Hey there, Rumpole! That girl's far too pretty for you to be dancing with.' At which the egregious

Proudfoot advanced on us and, with an arm round Daisy, turned her into the dancing position, a process to which, I was sorry to notice, she offered little or no resistance.

'That's as may be, Proudfoot—' I was anxious to keep the proceedings polite—'but Miss Sampson is *my* partner.'

'Not now,' he assured me. 'It's the "Gentlemen's Excuse Me" and we're fully entitled to carry off each other's partners. I suppose you don't go to many dances? You've got a lot to learn, Rumpole. A whole lot to learn.' At which the abominable prosecutor waltzed away with Daisy while the singer in the band repeated the verse I have quoted above.

I was walking moodily towards the bar when I heard another voice, clear as a bell but this time female, call, 'Rumpole!' I turned to see a fresh-faced and determined-looking young woman of my own age finishing an ice cream. I was, as I was so rarely to be in the future, temporarily lost for words.

'You *are* Rumpole, aren't you? I heard Reggie Proudfoot call you Rumpole.'

'Well, yes,' I had to concede, 'I am Rumpole.'

'I thought so! And you're in Daddy's chambers.'

'Daddy?' For a moment her description of our Head had me puzzled.

'I'm Hilda Wystan.' She gave a final lick to her ice-cream spoon and put it down on the glass plate. Little guessing what the future held, I said I was pleased to meet her, or made some such neutral remark.

'I like to keep my finger on the pulse of chambers,' she told me. 'I often drop in to see how

19

Daddy's managing you all. Albert tells me you're always before some Court of Petty Sessions. They must be keeping you pretty busy and you're not such a white wig after all. Although, come to think about it, you don't wear wigs in those inferior courts, do you? So your wig's probably as white as ever.'

I resolved to get hold of my wig and kick it around the dusty floor of the chambers' cellar until all its whiteness had gone for ever.

These thoughts were interrupted by Hilda Wystan. 'So, Rumpole, if you're so good at asking for things in front of the magistrates, aren't you going to ask me to dance?'

It was less a question than a command and I found myself obeying it. Hilda didn't laugh so much as Daisy, but she uttered sharp orders such as 'Left, left and left again' or 'We're coming up to the corner now, so *chassé*, Rumpole. Please remember to *chassé*!'

I saw Daisy Sampson laughing with Reggie Proudfoot's friends at the far end of the hall as I was steered through several more dance numbers by Hilda Wystan, including 'Jezebel' and 'Jealousy'. As we danced, I caught sight of a couple grasping hands and apparently throwing each other apart before pulling themselves together again. 'It's called "jiving", Rumpole,' Hilda Wystan, who seemed surprisingly up in these things, told me, 'but I wouldn't advise you to try it until you're better at the basic steps.'

As the band played 'Goodnight Irene', my friend Daisy came over to tell me that Reggie had agreed to drive her back to Dagenham because it was 'on his way home'—a statement which I didn't believe

20

to be true.

Not much later Hilda Wystan told me that 'Daddy' would be downstairs waiting to collect her, as he had been working late on a big brief in chambers. 'Never mind, Rumpole,' she said as she departed, 'we shall meet again. And it may be sooner than you expect.'

So I was left alone with a glass of dubious claret cup, in which leaves and slices of fruit floated, to wonder what Hilda Wystan had meant by her last doom-laden remark.

*   *   *

I didn't have long to wait for an answer. It was only a week or so later that C. H. Wystan came into the room where Uncle Tom was vainly trying to chip another golf ball into the wastepaper basket and I was making a note on yet another careless driving. He said, 'Would you care to dine, Rumpole?'

I was about to tell him that I only did so occasionally, when the Legal Aid cheques were paid in, but he went on, before I could interrupt, 'Just a family occasion. There'll be no need for you to dress.'

I had, I confess, a momentary temptation to ask, 'A naked family occasion?' but again I resisted it.

So I found myself, far earlier than I expected, ringing the front door bell of a grey house on a street of similar grey houses in Kensington. The door was opened by a maid as colourless and tidy as the house, with its grey wallpaper, framed etchings of views of the Swiss Alps and central heating kept economically at a low level. Without any preliminary drinking time, I found myself

21

facing the joint and two veg together with Wystan and his lady wife, a large anxious woman who seemed to be continually worried about the arrival and quality of the dinner.

'Oh, do stop worrying and calm down, Mother!' exclaimed Hilda. She clearly had little tolerance for her female parent. To her father she was far more patient, although she was noticeably better informed about the business of chambers than he was.

'It's true, isn't it, Daddy?' She seemed to be calling on his support as a mere formality. 'Albert likes the cut of Rumpole's jib? It's so important to get on well with the clerk.'

'Of course it's important.' C. H. Wystan was prepared to give a carefully balanced judgement on the subject. 'That doesn't mean that you have to join the clerk in the saloon bar or anything of that nature! That would not be in the fine tradition of the bar. Rumpole understands that, I'm sure.'

'Do you, Rumpole?' It was Hilda who asked the question.

'Oh, yes,' I was craven enough to agree. 'I understand it perfectly.' Youth is full of such small acts of betrayal. I promised myself to make it up to Albert the next time we met in Pommeroy's, a place of refuge from a harsh world.

When we had polished off the pudding (baked jam roll), C. H. Wystan gave a brief nod to his wife, who gathered up her daughter to depart. Before she left the room, Hilda said, 'Daddy's got some good news for you, Rumpole,' and she went off with what I can only describe as a smirk. I was surprised that what always seemed to me the barbaric custom of leaving men to port and dirty

22

jokes after the pud had then survived, even in the family circle, as one of the finest traditions of the bar.

Dirty jokes, of course, there were not. Port has always seemed to me a sickly sort of a wine, and I would have been happier with a glass of Pommeroy's Plonk with Albert than vintage Cockburn's with C. H. Wystan. 'Perhaps we shouldn't have given you Uncle Tom as a pupil master.' He seemed in an apologetic mood. 'He doesn't get much work.'

'He certainly doesn't.'

'All the same, he's a safe pair of hands.' It was then that I decided that, whatever became of me at the bar, I wouldn't be known simply for the safety of my hands.

'We had a fellow once in chambers. I never liked him. Name of Denver. Well, Denver had a pupil from whom he extracted the usual £100 fee. And do you know, the very next day after he'd got it, Denver and our junior clerk legged it over to France! We never saw hide nor hair of either of them again. Horrible business, this Penge Bungalow affair, don't you think? Pure evil. A fellow shooting his father.' His small beady eyes peered out in horror as though amazed at such examples of the wickedness of the world in both cases. They were definitely not in the finest traditions of the bar.

However, there was one of these traditions that, although I was young, insecure and drinking his port wine, I felt I had to recall to C. H. Wystan's attention. 'We don't *know* that your client in the Penge Bungalow affair shot his father, do we? I mean, we shan't know that until the jury comes

23

back with a verdict of guilty.'

Hilda's daddy looked at me and his expression was pained. As though to cover his embarrassment, he said, 'Things look very black against him. Very black indeed.'

'That's before you've tested the evidence.'

'I shall go through all the motions, Rumpole, in the best tradition of our great profession. But I can't hold out any high hopes for the wretched boy, I'm afraid. I can't hold out very much hope for him at all.'

'I haven't read the evidence.'

'No, Rumpole. Of course you haven't. Perhaps you will have that opportunity at some future time. At the moment all we can say is that public opinion—that is, the opinion of any jury—is likely to be dead against young Jerold.'

'So he's a client who desperately needs defending brilliantly,' was what I should have said. Being young and, as I say, craven, I only managed, 'I'm sure you'll have difficulties.'

'I won't have difficulties, Rumpole.' Here Wystan let a note of sadness in. 'I will have impossibilities! Two war heroes murdered, men who saved our nation. A couple of "the few" who went on fearless bombing raids.'

I swallowed a sweet and sticky gulp of port and became bold enough to say, 'Weren't "the few" *fighter* pilots?'

'Men shot down over occupied France who managed to get back to England at the end of the war.' Wystan ignored my interruption. 'Victims of an apparently completely senseless shooting by the boy Simon Jerold.'

'Would you rather he'd shot a couple of

conscientious objectors?' was what I felt I ought to have said. Once again, for reasons of youth, I didn't.

'My daughter, Hilda, as you may have noticed,' C. H. Wystan seemed to have felt there was no more to be said on the subject of murder and our attention should be turned to more important matters, 'takes a lively interest in all that is going on in chambers. She was appointed a school monitor at an unusually early age.'

I did my best to look suitably impressed.

Wystan continued, 'Now, as you probably know, I've been offered the leading brief in *R. v. Jerold* by a perfectly decent firm of solicitors in Penge.'

'Albert told me that.' I tried as hard as I could to keep the note of hopeless envy out of my voice.

'I am telling you, Rumpole. It might be better if you waited for me to give you the news rather than pick up tittle-tattle from the clerk's room. The point is that in this case the solicitors have taken the rather unusual step of asking me to nominate a junior, from our chambers of course.'

'Of course,' I repeated. I felt another twinge of envy at the luck of some other, older member of number 4 Equity Court.

'It was Hilda who put your name forward. She said, "Why not give young Rumpole a chance to prove himself, Daddy?" She always calls me Daddy, you know.' He sounded more pleased than apologetic.

'Yes,' I told him, 'I know.' The pang of envy had become a rush of adrenalin. This drained away like used bathwater as C. H. Wystan made my terms of employment clear. 'You'll be expected to take a full note of the evidence and look up any points of law that may arise. But you're not to worry, Rumpole. I shan't expect you to deal with witnesses, or indeed open your mouth at any point in the trial.'

5

For the first time in my legal career my brief contained photographs of a dead man. 'Jerry' Jerold had been found by the police photographer, sitting in a chair in the bungalow's living room. Behind him was the door which opened on to a narrow hallway. You could see the corner of the mantelpiece and part of Jerry's collection of war memorabilia. The man in the chair looked still at his ease: his Brylcreemed hair was neatly brushed back, his glazed eyes seemed to express nothing but mild surprise. He wore a blazer with flannel trousers and an RAF tie. Only the dark stain on his shirt, spreading across his chest, indicated the cause of death.

'Making a note for your learned leader in that Jerold case, are you?' Uncle Tom placed a golf ball carefully on the carpet and appeared to threaten it with his golf club.

'Making a note for myself, as a matter of fact,' was what I longed to tell him, but didn't yet have the courage.

In the last photograph Jerry was naked on a mortuary slab, his hair still neatly in place as though glued. I turned to the prosecution witness statements, the account of how he arrived, after missing death in the skies during the war, at this final humiliating end. The story was told in the greatest detail by Pilot Officer Peter Benson, who had been at the reunion party and gone back with Jerry to his bungalow at Penge.

They had met, a dozen of them in all, including

Peter and 'Tail-End' Charlie, in the bar of the Cafe Royal. By the time they got to the Palladium they were not entirely sober and 'Tail-End' insisted on joining Judy Garland in her songs. After the theatre they had a few more drinks at a bar near Victoria Station and they all arrived at Jerry's bungalow just before midnight.

Young Simon Jerold was in bed and asleep when they got there, but his father woke him up and set him to making tea and pouring more drinks for the old companions of the war in the air. Jerry, Peter Benson insisted, was 'getting at' his son, telling him to drink a couple of large whiskies like a man and letting the assembled company know that his son not only had no idea what a war was like but had funked his national service.

'The boy's more scared of his sergeant on the parade ground than ever we were of German fighters,' Jerry apparently said. It was then, it seemed, that the boy had lost his temper. Benson remembered him 'shouting his mouth off' and telling his father, 'National service is ridiculous, there isn't going to be another war anyway.' Simon also said, 'What's the point of wasting your youth learning how to kill people?' and announced he wasn't going back to his army station anyway.

At this point the war survivors were indignant, there was a cry of 'go for his trousers', which seemed to indicate that some sort of debagging or other humiliation was intended, and Simon picked up the German pistol from the mantelpiece and pointed it at his father, saying, to the best of Benson's recollection, 'You're so keen on teaching people to kill people. I promise you I'll kill the first of you that touches me. So you'd better watch out.'

28

This threat, uttered by a hysterical boy holding a pistol, seemed to have produced an unusual silence from his tormentors, during which it was Benson who went up to Simon and took the gun out of his hand. The boy released it and immediately went back into his bedroom, banging the door.

After this the party continued for some time before the revellers went to their homes. It wasn't until next morning that Simon rang the police to tell them that he had woken up to find his father dead in a chair. Joan Plumpton, a cleaning lady who worked at both bungalows, opened 'Tail-End' Charlie's door at nine-thirty to find him lying in the small hallway also shot through the heart. A German bullet was found in the bodies of the two wartime companions and the Luger pistol, having been recently fired, was found in a dustbin outside Jerry's bungalow. That, in brief, was the story of the Penge Bungalow Murders.

'I shouldn't waste too much of your time over that bundle of papers, my boy.' Uncle Tom had just failed to chip his golf ball into the wastepaper basket. 'From what I've read about it you've got no defence.'

'I think we have,' I was now bold enough to answer. 'It's called the presumption of innocence.'

'I don't think that's going to get you very far, to be honest.'

I had a gloomy feeling that he was probably right. All the same, I went across to the library and tried to find some comfort in the forensic science book (this was in the days before my old friend Professor Ackerman had composed his great work), and I read every word concerning gunshot wounds, the effect of bleeding and the time of

29

death. I was still reading when the daylight dimmed and the man with the flaming rod was round to light the lamps, and still I hadn't found any satisfactory answer to our problem.

*   *   *

I had been in prisons before, of course, visiting minor villains involved in more or less trivial offences. I hadn't met anyone accused of murder in the Scrubs or seen the pride mixed with a kind of awe with which wardens produce a star prisoner, in this case the boy accused of patricide and double murder who was featured in the pages of the *News of the World.* When he was brought into the interview room he seemed remote, like a spirit on its way to becoming disembodied. He was wearing prison clothes at least a couple of sizes too large for his slim body. He had his father's good looks but softened, almost feminine, and no brilliantine controlled his bright, straying hair. He hardly raised his eyes to us but sat staring at his hands, which he held crossed in his lap, as though wondering if they could have been guilty of two violent crimes.

The room was bleak, furnished with a plain wooden table at which Simon Jerold's legal team all sat. C. H. Wystan was at the head of the table, wearing what was, even for him, a particularly sombre look. With the tips of his fingers touching and his hands steepled, he was about to forget he was there as an advocate and became a judge. I, the young Rumpole, was beside him, having supplied him with the detailed notes I wasn't sure he had read.

30

Further down the table, as it might be under the salt, was our instructing solicitor, Barnsley Gough, who carried on his business at Penge and congratulated himself on being sharp. Indeed most of what he said was calculated to show how sharp he was. He had sharp features, a particularly sharp nose and a small bristling moustache that looked as though it might draw blood at a touch. He came with a clerk, almost a boy, who looked as young as, if not younger than, our client, whom he called Bernard, with a distinct emphasis on the second syllable, so I didn't know if it was a first or second name. I did notice, however, that it was Bernard who was able to find any documents in a bundle with which Barnsley Gough seemed surprisingly unfamiliar.

Our client sat apart from us, isolated on a chair in the middle of the room, under a light which was there to help out the grey end of a rainy late afternoon.

'I think we're all agreed, Jerold,' Wystan summed up the situation, 'that it's going to be extremely difficult to provide a successful defence in your particular case.'

It was then that Simon looked up, and I saw the terror in his eyes that I could still remember so many decades later in a chambers meeting.

'But I didn't do it.' His voice was so weak it was almost a whisper. 'I never shot Dad or Charlie.'

'You were heard to threaten your father with the gun. A number of witnesses saw that, you know.' Wystan said this slowly, again as though explaining a complicated situation to an errant child.

'But I never shot Dad. I never did it.'

'You've told us that.' Barnsley Gough took over

31

the role of a patient teacher. 'And of course we have to accept what you say. But it's the evidence! That's what I've had to explain to you. The evidence is dead against you. What Mr Wystan is trying to tell you—and, as you know, Mr Wystan has enormous experience of these matters—' here my leader gave a brief but learned nod—'Mr Wystan takes the view that the evidence is so black against us that we must . . . well, we must . . .' Here our instructing solicitor, for all his sharpness, balked at mentioning the terrible conclusion.

'You must be prepared,' Wystan took over the proceedings, 'for the worst. It's my duty to give you that warning.'

Simon seemed genuinely puzzled. 'Aren't you here to defend me?'

'Of course I am.' Wystan looked pained. 'And rest assured, I shall take every point in your favour, in the fine tradition of the bar. It's my duty to warn you, that's all. Now, I suppose I can tell the jury you loved your father?'

'Once I loved him. Sometimes I hardly liked him at all.' I could see that we had a client with a possibly fatal tendency to tell the truth.

'Then I shan't ask that question.' Wystan was making a note, but when Simon went on he stopped writing.

'He was always shouting at Mum when she was alive. She cried a lot. He made her cry.'

'You're not going to be asked that, so don't go into details,' Barnsley Gough tried to stop him sharply, but Simon went on, 'It seemed like he couldn't forgive me for not being old enough to get killed in the war.'

'We had considered,' Wystan was naturally

32

anxious to change the subject, 'trying to prove insanity.'

'Dad was insane.' For once Simon seemed to agree with his defender. 'Filling the bungalow with all those relics of death.'

'Mr Wystan was referring to your state of mind, Jerold,' Gough explained patiently. 'We considered guilty but insane, but the doctors wouldn't play ball. Unfortunately they gave you high marks for intelligence.'

'So we are thrown back on the facts.' Wystan was resigned.

Our client looked out of the window to see, in the early shadows, dogs patrolling the prison yard, and then at the door, where the back view of a warder filled the glass panel. I guessed he would have done anything he could to escape having to repeat the story he had told so often without finding anyone to believe him.

As he did so, I did my best to picture the scene. The resentful boy hounded out of bed in his pyjamas and dressing gown to wait on the half-drunken group of his father's friends. As he did so, he admitted, he poured himself a couple of furtive but large whiskies, which fuelled his anger when his father attacked him, and he picked up the Luger. I tried to imagine the flushed, suddenly alarmed faces of the wartime heroes as the boy's hand shook and he turned towards his father.

'Did you say, "I promise you I'll kill the first of you that touches me"?' Wystan was going through Simon's statement to the police, producing nothing new or surprising.

'They were going to do something . . . pull my trousers off or something. Charlie was the worst.'

'Were they all threatening you?'

'Practically all. I think one of them said, "Leave the boy alone."'

'Really? Which one was that?' I heard myself asking.

'His name was Harry. Harry Daniels.'

I made a note on my brief.

'Then what happened?' Wystan didn't seem best pleased with my interruption.

'I told Dad that if he was so keen on teaching people to kill people, he'd better watch out.'

'You admit that?' Wystan sadly underlined part of the statement.

'The client admits all that.' Gough encouraged the underlining. 'And that he had the gun pointed at his father.'

'Until you were relieved of it by whom?' I asked.

'Ex-Pilot Officer Benson.'

I was only trying to be helpful but Wystan sighed even more heavily. 'Thank you, Rumpole. I can read the prosecution statements. Yes, please go on, Jerold.'

So we heard how Simon went back to bed after he'd been disarmed and slept heavily. Something woke him in the night, but he'd gone to sleep to the sound of the party and, still dazed by whisky, he thought it was the party continuing. He woke up at about six with a dry mouth and got up for a drink of water. On his way to the kitchen he saw his father dead in the chair, the bloodstain on his shirt spread across his chest.

'What did you do then?' Wystan asked.

'I got dressed and left the bungalow.'

'What time was that?'

'About six-thirty. It was just starting to get light.'

'Why didn't you call for help for your father? Why didn't you call the police?'

'I thought I'd get the blame because of what happened with the gun. They'd think I'd done it.'

'You were right there anyway, my lad!' Barnsley Gough couldn't resist it.

'Yes, I was. I walked round for a bit and then I thought they'd pick me up in the end so I'd better tell them what had happened. That was when I rang the police.'

'Did you go to Charlie Weston's bungalow during the night?'

'Not at all.'

'Did you shoot the man Weston in his bungalow?'

'Never. I promise you I never shot either of them.'

There was a long silence. Then my leader hammered another nail in Simon's coffin. 'You do realize that your failure to call for an ambulance or the police when you saw your father dead adds considerably to our difficulties. You would agree with that, Mr Gough, I'm sure?'

'I certainly would.' Barnsley Gough was quick to answer. 'It's the stumbling block, as you might say. You must realize that, my lad.'

'You mean, you can't help me?' Simon had been surprisingly calm when he was telling his story. Now the terror had returned and he looked at his leading counsel, who was saying nothing. In this silence, I heard my voice, it seemed from far away, asking a question.

'When you found your father dead, where was the German gun?'

'Nowhere. I mean, I didn't see it anywhere.'

35

Simon was looking at me now, and answered my question with a kind of hope.

'It wasn't with the rest of the war museum on the mantelpiece?'

'I don't think so. I didn't really look.'

'And two bullets had been fired, Mr Rumpole.' Our solicitor spoke as though explaining the basic facts of the case to someone who could never be as sharp as himself. 'The expert evidence tells us that.'

'Yes, I know it does. What I want to ask you,' I tried to speak to Simon Jerold as though we were alone in the room, 'is, did you wipe your fingerprints off the gun and the magazine?'

'I never did that.'

'What are you suggesting, Rumpole?' Again my leader didn't sound altogether pleased by my interruption. 'Who says they were wiped off?'

'Forensic science report,' I said, and Bernard, the young office boy, supplied the reference. 'Page 56 of the depositions.'

Wystan looked it up reluctantly and then rebuked me. 'The gun and magazine had evidently been wiped. There were no fingerprints of any sort.'

'Exactly!' I told him.

'In any event, everyone had seen our client holding the gun. What would have been the point of his wiping off his own fingerprints?'

'That was the question I felt sure you'd want to ask,' I told Wystan, hoping I sounded respectful.

'Well, Jerold. Did you wipe the handle of the gun to remove fingerprints?'

'No, sir. Never.'

'That's your answer, Rumpole. I know you were trying to help.' Then Wystan turned to the client with what I supposed he thought were consoling words. 'Mr Rumpole, Jerold, is, like yourself, a young man. But *you're* not to worry. Mr Rumpole will be a great help to me by taking a full note of the evidence. But all the questions will be asked by me and I will, of course, make the final speech to the jury on your behalf. Now, does that set your mind at rest?'

Simon Jerold didn't look as though his mind was at rest. He gazed at me as though I had asked a new question which might, just possibly, supply some sort of chink of light in the darkness which surrounded him. But Wystan hadn't entirely finished with young Simon, and he seemed, at last, ready to sound a more positive note.

'As far as your father's case is concerned—' Wystan looked up to the ceiling as he spoke, as though seeking inspiration from heaven—'it would help if he had threatened you again, perhaps attacked you when you got up to get water from the kitchen. We might, might we not, Mr Barnsley Gough, go for provocation?'

'Seems about the only thing we could go for. I agree with Mr Wystan,' our sharp solicitor told Simon.

'It would only reduce murder to manslaughter, of course. But we might avoid the worst consequence.' Wystan seemed shy of mentioning the great obscenity, hanging by the neck.

'I've put this to you, Simon, haven't I? That he attacked you and that's why you shot him?' Barnsley Gough had been, apparently, one step ahead of my leader.

'He couldn't have attacked me.' Simon sighed, as though tired of explaining a simple fact. 'He was

37

dead. And I never shot him, never!' Was this a client, I wondered, who refused to tell a lie even in the hope of saving his life?

'Mr Wystan,' Barnsley Gough was persistent, 'is only suggesting what might have happened.'

'Well, it didn't!' Simon was equally persistent. 'I'm quite sure of that.'

'What will happen,' Wystan gave us his idea of a smooth solution to a difficult problem, 'is that we shall listen to all the evidence about the party and the medical evidence. We really don't need to challenge any of it. And then, when the time comes for him to give evidence, our client may have a clearer memory of the events of that terrible night. In the fullness of time.'

At which Simon only repeated, 'I never shot him.' And the conference was over.

On my way back to the Temple I said to C. H. Wystan, 'So you wanted him to say his father attacked him in the night?' Suggesting this story hadn't seemed, I had to admit, in strict accordance with the finest traditions of the bar.

My leader, however, was unashamed. 'He may remember that's what happened in the fullness of time,' he said.

'How does that fit in with Charlie Weston's murder? Are we suggesting Simon went round to his bungalow and got attacked by him too?'

'He may remember more about that. You'll have to rely on me to conduct this case in my own way, unless you can suggest a better sort of defence.'

I had to confess that I couldn't, although I made a silent vow to do so. In the fullness of time.

6

'You should sit, best part of the day, Mr Rumpole, with your leg elevated.'

'That's quite impossible.'

'Of course it's not impossible. Just get a low stool, put a cushion on it and elevate your leg. It doesn't require great athletic skill.'

I had visited Dr McClintock, our local quack, on my wife Hilda's (known to me only as She Who Must Be Obeyed) often repeated insistence. Check-ups are, in my experience, a grave mistake; all they do is allow the quack of your choice to tell you that you have some sort of complaint that you were far happier not knowing about. Or else they prescribe some totally impossible course of conduct, as was the case with McClintock, who looked at me as though I might soon become a blank space on his National Health list.

'Why on earth should you want me to do that?' I asked.

'Because,' McClintock spoke very slowly as though explaining the secrets of the universe to a small halfwit, 'it'll be good for your circulation.'

'It may be good for my circulation, but it'll be extremely bad for my practice at the bar.'

'I'm not sure I'm quite clear what you mean, Mr Rumpole.' He was puzzled but tolerant, as though the halfwit had started to babble.

'Do you think I could address a jury with my leg elevated? Could I cross-examine with my foot in the air?'

'Mr Rumpole, I don't think you quite

understand . . .'

'You don't think I understand?' By now the quack had touched a nerve. He had challenged all I had learned from a lifetime's experience ever since . . . well, ever since the case which confirmed me as a force to be reckoned with down the Old Bailey. 'Do you imagine,' I asked the final question that would blow his medical theories to the winds, 'do you honestly imagine that I could have done the Penge Bungalow Murders, alone and without a leader, but with one leg cocked up on a joint stool?'

'I'm not concerned with how many murders you might have done in the suburbs of London, Mr Rumpole. I'm concerned about your circulation.'

It was to escape the rule of the eccentric Dr McClintock, and to be able to write with both feet firmly planted on the ground, that I took my memoirs down to chambers and started to write in my room there. I was about to have another great remembrance of things past, when my sweet silent thoughts were interrupted by a brisk knock at the door and the entrance of a personable young lady carrying a mug which she put down carefully on the corner of my *Archbold on Criminal Law and Procedure*.

'Albert told me black with no sugar. Is that how you like it, Mr Rumpole?'

'That's exactly how I like it. Do you work for any of our solicitors?' I was hoping she might be bringing a brief to go with the coffee.

'Afraid not. I'm Lala Ingolsby, Liz Probert's pupil. She told me you know more about the practice of the criminal law than anyone in the Temple.'

'That's strictly true.'

40

'So she's sure you can give me some excellent advice.'

'Possibly.' I took out a small cigar to go with the coffee. 'Do you mind?' I remembered to say as I struck a match.

'Not at all. In fact I rather like it.'

I began to warm to this Lala Ingolsby.

'What's that you're working on now?' Lala was inspecting the pieces of virgin paper, across which that day my pen had scarcely travelled.

'My memoirs. I am recalling the Penge Bungalow Murders. You won't have heard of the case.'

'Wasn't that the one about the two ex-air force officers found shot?'

'You know that?' Lala's approval rating continued to rise.

'Oh, yes, we had books at home called *Notable British Trials*. You were in that case, weren't you?'

'When my wig was as white as yours, Miss Ingolsby.'

'And you did it without a leader?'

'It was all a long time ago.'

'How can I get into a case like that?'

'You'll have to wait until someone gets killed in an interesting way in the suburbs. Then get led by your Head of Chambers.'

'By Mr Ballard?'

Soapy Sam, I thought, would make an excellent lost leader, but I resisted the temptation of pointing this out to my new-found and young learned friend. All I said was, 'Someone with Sam Ballard's qualities, yes.'

Lala thought this over and said, 'There's something else I'd like your advice about.'

41

'You probably need my advice on the subject of bloodstains?'

'It's not bloodstains. It's Claude Erskine-Brown.'

Again I resisted the temptation to say, 'Much the same thing.' So I said, 'Liz Probert has reported him to the Society of Women Barristers. Re the matter of your legs.'

'I didn't really mind that. It's just that he keeps on about it. And quite honestly I don't fancy Erskine-Brown.'

'Quite honestly,' I had to admit, 'neither do I.'

'I know Liz got excited about it. I just want him to stop. It's become embarrassing.'

'Embarrassing to have him making flattering remarks about your personal appearance?'

'Well, it is. Quite honestly.'

'And you want him to stop?'

'Quite honestly, yes. What do you think I ought to do, Mr Rumpole? You've had so much experience of life.'

'A life of crime,' I had to admit.

'So what should I do?'

'You really want to stop Claude dead in his tracks?'

'That sort of thing, yes.'

'Then tell him you love him passionately. Tell him you want him to get a divorce and marry you. Above all, tell him you're going to ring up Mrs Justice Erskine-Brown, once the Portia of our chambers and my long-ago pupil, now married to Claude.'

'Why should I want to ring her up?'

'Tell him it's to beg her to set him free because you can't live without each other.'

'What do you think will happen if I tell him all

42

that?'

'I think he'll run a mile. I think he'll drop your legs as a topic of conversation. I think he'll never speak to you as you're standing by the notice board again.'

'It's not very flattering to think he'd react like that.'

'It may well not be flattering, but it'll work,' and I added, in words she could understand, 'quite honestly.'

'I suppose I might try it.' At which she left me, grinning broadly.

I no longer thought of what havoc I might have wreaked on the love lives of the present members of our chambers. I picked up my pen and dived back in time to the days when my wig was as white as Miss Lala Ingolsby's. I summed up the situation and carried on my narrative in the following way.

*   *   *

Looking back at Equity Court in the days when C. H. Wystan was our Head and Uncle Tom was chipping golf balls into the wastepaper basket, I miss the figures who have become so much a part of my life and seem inseparable from the building. Claude Erskine-Brown had not arrived to bore us about his nights at the opera and fall hopelessly in love at least once a month, nor had our Portia, Phillida Trant, who remarkably married him. Guthrie Featherstone, QC, MP, was still to take us over and Soapy Sam Ballard was organizing debates among his fellow law students on such subjects as 'Is adultery a quasi-criminal offence?' and 'A Christian approach to smoking'.

Most of the members of chambers at the time of the Penge Bungalow affair have died or become judges or, in other ways, put an end to their active lives. Their faces, plump and self-satisfied or sharp-nosed and inquisitive, have drifted into that great gallery of past learned friends I have been against and judges I have found irritating. Little labels which might have given me a clue as to their names and identities have got rubbed smooth and become illegible over the course of the years.

A character who sticks in my mind, however, and had some influence on events surrounding the Penge Bungalow affair, was Teddy Singleton. He was by far the most elegant member of Equity Court. He lived in South Kensington with someone he always referred to as 'Mumsie' and rarely left chambers without putting on a fawn overcoat with a velvet collar and carrying a tightly rolled umbrella. He spoke in a voice which, having hit on an effective note of amused contempt, was disinclined to try any change of expression.

Uncle Tom, defeated by the wastepaper basket, had drifted off home and the gas lights were being lit. I sat on in our room, turning the pages of the forensic science book, trying not to look at the photographs of battered babies and strangled women, but to concentrate on the information to be gained from bloodstains and the spattering of blood, making a note which I hoped C. H. Wystan would find useful. Teddy Singleton glided into the room and asked me what I was doing. I was good enough to tell him but he dismissed my efforts with a short, staccato burst of laughter.

'Don't worry your pretty little head about that, Rumpole. You might think you've got an important job. Case in the public eye. Head of Chambers leading you. I tell you, I've been led by Wystan and he won't even let his junior read out an agreed statement.'

'I'm just seeing if we can get anything from the blood.'

'Don't worry your pretty little head.' It was the sort of remark that would get Erskine-Brown in trouble with the sisterhood these days, and it seemed peculiarly inappropriate when applied to me, as he soon realized. Teddy gave me a more critical examination. 'Your head's not exactly pretty, is it? All the same, I'm going to offer you a speaking part. Dear old con, spent half his life in chokey, so it won't come as much of a shock to him. I can't do it. I'm in a fun divorce case across the road.'

'You mean he's pleading guilty?' My interest in Teddy's brief was already shrinking. 'Why's he doing that?'

'You think you'll find that rather dull? Never mind. It doesn't much matter what you say. You could say this isn't a case of juvenile crime. It's elderly, non-violent and extremely unsuccessful crime. You could ask the court to take into consideration the fact that your client is one of the most unsuccessful burglars who ever failed to break and enter a fish and chip shop with the door left open. Anyway, I'm giving you the opportunity. Aren't you going to thank me?'

'If I'm supposed to,' I conceded.

'Of course you are! Life's not all junior briefs in sensational murders, you know.' At which Teddy Singleton went off, swinging his rolled umbrella, to his 'fun divorce case' or some other source of

45

entertainment. In due course I got the brief from Albert in *R*. v. *Timson*. At that time the name meant nothing to me.

After Singleton had left me, I decided it was time I let my learned leader know my thoughts on the bloodstains in *R*. v. *Jerold*. I trudged along to his room, knocked at the door and was invited to come in by a commanding but strangely high-pitched voice. As I did so, I was greeted with the spectacle of Hilda seated comfortably behind her father's desk, filing her nails and reading a magazine.

'Hello there, Rumpole!' She called to me as though she was hailing some small ship in difficulties from the comparative safety of the shore. 'I thought I might bump into you again while I was here. I'm waiting for Daddy to come back from court and take me out to dinner. Got any particular message for him, have you?'

'Blood.' I tried to put the matter as shortly as possible.

'What's blood got to do with it?'

'It's about the bloodstains in the Penge Bungalow affair.'

'Well, of course there were bloodstains, Daddy knows that, if that wretched boy shot his father.'

'*If* he did? We have to presume he didn't do it.'

'Why on earth should we presume that?' Hilda Wystan was giving me her look of tolerant amusement.

'Because the law tells us to.'

I suppose I was being pompous, but she smiled tolerantly and said, 'The presumption of innocence doesn't mean that some people aren't guilty.'

The Wystan daughter had a point there, but I

46

didn't want to give her the satisfaction of admitting it. So I said, 'If you could just tell your father that I've had some ideas about the blood.'

'Oh, I don't think Daddy'll be very interested in ideas about the blood.'

'Perhaps you could tell me what part of the defence does interest your daddy?' I thought of that terrified boy, alone in a cell, expecting death, and I have to confess to a distinct rise in the supply of righteous indignation.

'Daddy always says that the job of a defending counsel is to wrap the client in a cloak of respectability,' Hilda told me.

'I just happen to believe that bloodstains might be more useful to Simon than a cloak of respectability.'

'Who's Simon?'

'Young Simon. The prisoner at the bar.'

'Daddy calls him "Jerold". I don't think he's ever referred to him as "Simon".'

'Perhaps he should. Then the jury might think of him as a human being. A boy. Perhaps they've got sons his age.' Although, of course, I had never done a murder trial, I had given the matter a good deal of serious thought.

'Rumpole!' My learned leader's daughter stopped me as though I was a runaway pony, galloping completely out of control. 'I think for your future career, after *R*. v. *Jerold*'s over of course, you should concentrate on the civil law.'

'Civil law? I hardly know any civil law.' It was true: I had scraped through contract after a humiliating retake.

'Then I think you should brush up on it, Rumpole. Daddy always says that civil law is so

47

much cleaner than crime.'

'I don't agree,' I had no hesitation in telling her.

'Don't you, Rumpole?' She still looked at me in an amused sort of way, as though I was a young but harmless eccentric.

'To me criminal law is all about life, love and the pursuit of happiness. Civil law's only about money, an uninteresting subject.' It was a sentence I had used in one of my examination papers to cover my profound ignorance of the rules governing bills of exchange.

'Do you really think money an uninteresting subject, Rumpole?' Hilda's tolerant smile was now a permanent fixture. 'You'll probably think differently when it comes to getting married.'

'If I ever do, I'm sure I'll be able to rub along on a life of crime,' I was unwise enough to tell her.

'Rubbing along doesn't sound quite good enough, Rumpole. I'm sure your wife will expect more than that. By the way, you know how you landed the junior brief in *R. v. Jerold*?'

'Your father said,' I remembered the conversation over the Wystan port, 'that you recommended me.'

'I did, Rumpole. You can be sure that, when it comes to questions of your career, I have your interests at heart.'

The telephone rang then and I gathered it was Daddy, telling his daughter to meet him for dinner at Simpson's in the Strand. Hilda departed in a hurry and I was left worrying more about the bloodstains in the Penge bungalows and less than perhaps I should about why Hilda Wystan was planning my future career at the bar. In my comparative innocence, I hadn't noticed that the dark clouds were gathering not only over Simon Jerold but over much of Rumpole's life to come.

7

'It's quite like old times,' Daisy Sampson said as we were dealing with a late breakfast (bun and butter washed down by watery coffee) in the canteen at London Sessions as a prelude to a visit to my client, Cyril Timson, in the cells in order to search for some more or less lovable act to mitigate the effects of his confession of guilt.

'Yes,' I said, 'the old times before you danced away from me.'

I tried not to sound bitter, and Daisy drew back the scarlet lips on her slightly protuberant teeth and gave me a brilliant smile. 'That was only a bit of fun,' she started to mitigate for herself. 'That was the "Gentlemen's Excuse Me".'

'That gentleman excused himself far too much, if you want my opinion.'

'Well, you weren't alone for long. That other girl seemed dead keen to dance with you.'

'That "other girl", as you call her, happens to be the daughter of my Head of Chambers.'

'Well, that didn't stop her being dead keen on dancing with you.'

I bit into my bun. What Daisy had just said seemed to point to a road down which I was not yet prepared to travel. I was determined to return the conversation to the safer subject of crime.

'Anyway, you sent the brief to Teddy Singleton.'

'When he couldn't do it, I suggested he passed it on to you.'

'Thank you, Daisy.' I supposed a brief was a fair substitute for a dance.

51

'I thought it would be good for you to meet the Timsons.'

'There's more than one of them?'

'Oh, a huge number. They're great on family values. Look, over there, they've all turned up to see Uncle Cyril sent back to prison. They reckon he needs a lot of support.'

She nodded towards a table in the corner at which a number of respectable-looking citizens of various ages and sexes were talking in quiet, concerned voices and drinking coffee.

'They look a reliable group,' I said. 'Shall I call some of them as character witnesses?'

'Better not.'

'Why?'

'They've all got more convictions than you've had hot dinners, Horace.'

'What do they do?'

'Crime. Oh, no violence. Nothing spectacular. Just ordinary, decent breaking and entering, that sort of thing. That's why they look so respectable. But the best thing about them is they provide an enormous amount of work for the legal profession.'

It was when she said this that I was prepared to forgive Daisy her infidelity at the Inner Temple ball. 'If that's the case,' I said, 'let's not hang about here. Let's go straight down and talk to Uncle Cyril.'

*   *   *

'The charge is that you broke into Sound Universe, in spite of its title a comparatively small radio and television shop in Coldharbour Lane, at two in the morning of 3 March and stole six radios, one

52

television set, five alarm clocks, four electric kettles, oh, and one small egg-timer.'

'Two o'clock in the morning, is that what it says?' Uncle Cyril was short and plump with greying hair. I judged him to be in his sixties. He smiled a lot, seemed grateful for my visit and was clearly amused by the time the burglary had allegedly taken place.

'Yes,' I assured him. 'It was a night-time job.'

'But two in the morning! I never been out of bed at two in the morning! Never in my life. Why've they put that in? It's just silly.'

'Presumably it's because that's when Mr Rochford says he saw you putting the stuff in your van . . .'

'Van?' Uncle Cyril seemed even more amused. 'I haven't got a van. Not one that's roadworthy anyway.'

A great wave of relief had come over me. We were going to have a fight on our hands, a battle in court, during which I intended to startle Daisy and the hard-working Timson family with my brilliance. C. H. Wystan may have condemned me to silence in the Penge Bungalow affair, but I had a chance of winning the Queen against Uncle Cyril, alone and without a leader.

'So you want to plead not guilty?' I was prepared to take formal instructions from the client.

'Guilty!'

'What?' Had I heard him correctly?

'I'm going to say guilty.'

'But if you were in bed and you haven't got a van that works, why on earth . . . ?'

'Because it's safer.'

'You'll be sent back to prison.'

53

'That,' Uncle Cyril was no longer smiling, 'will be much safer.'

'What are you talking about?'

Uncle Cyril answered with a single word: 'Molloys.'

As our conversation had wandered into paths I no longer understood, I turned to Daisy for help.

'The Molloys,' she explained the mystery, 'and the Timsons hate each other.'

'Who are these Molloys?'

'Another big family in the same south London patch. The Molloys, on the whole, do crime that's neither ordinary nor decent.'

'Too right,' Uncle Cyril added, while I suggested, 'Violent and unusual?'

'You've got it,' Daisy assured me.

'The Molloys won't forgive me over the Meadowsweet Building Society job.'

'What was that?' I now asked Daisy.

'The offices got robbed. And one of the Molloys was arrested.'

'It was Jimmy Molloy. And I happened to mention his name to "Persil" White,' Uncle Cyril told me.

' "Persil"?' Again I turned to my interpreter for assistance.

'Detective Inspector White. He's always telling people he's whiter than white, so they've named him after a soap powder,' Daisy explained.

'I happened to bump into "Persil" down the Needle Arms and he said, "You got anything for me, Cyril?" '

'He wanted an alarm clock?' I asked. In my salad days I still had a lot to learn.

'No, I guess he wanted information, didn't he,

54

Cyril?' Daisy asked our client.

'Too right he did.'

'And I suppose you gave him a few titbits?'

'I know it's not right. Of course I do. But I'm getting too old for all this breaking and entering, across roofs and stuff. And I've got to an age when I prefer my bed of a night-time. So I'm glad of a bit of regular income.'

'And what did you tell "Persil" this time?' Daisy asked.

'I just happened to mention, casual, that there was talk of Jimmy Molloy in connection with the Meadowsweet job.'

'For which Jimmy got three years, if I remember.' Once again Daisy revealed her encyclopedic knowledge of the affairs of the criminal classes in the south Brixton area.

'So they give me the Sound Universe as a bit, like, of revenge.'

'Who gave it to you?' I felt it was time I took charge of the conference.

'Well, the Molloys, you see. Course it was one of them fingering me to "Persil" in the Needle Arms. I can't fight them, Mr Rumpole. Not at my age. I can't do battle with them, not the Molloys.'

'But if you didn't do it?'

'Of course I didn't do it, but they'll get me anyway. That's why I want to go inside. I'll be much safer there.'

'Can I get this clear?' I needed to be sure, because I had serious doubts about Uncle Cyril's sanity. 'You *want* to go to prison?'

'Safest place for me, Mr Rumpole. I reckons I'll be looked after there. I'm used to it, of course. Reckon I'll get Wandsworth. Jimmy Molloy got sent up north somewhere.'

'So in order to get to what you regard as safety in prison, you're ready to plead guilty to a crime you didn't commit?'

'Seems the only way, Mr Rumpole. They don't let you into them places, not just by kicking at the door and asking if they got any cells to spare.'

'And you tell me you never broke into the radio shop in Coldharbour Lane?'

'Never. At any time!'

'Then I can't do it.'

'Can't do what, Mr Rumpole?'

'Let you plead guilty.' The finest traditions of the bar, whatever they were, seemed at that moment a lot more important than the exact shade of trousers to wear when addressing the Court of Appeal.

'That's my business, isn't it, what I admits to?'

'We're here to take the client's instructions, aren't we?' Daisy seemed to think I was being unnecessarily difficult.

'The world is full,' I told her from the mountains, or at least the molehill, of my experience, 'of stories about barristers who defend people they know are guilty. I absolutely refuse to be the first barrister who's pleaded guilty for a customer he knows is innocent. However attractive you find the idea of prison, Mr Timson.'

'You reckon I ought to fight it?' Uncle Cyril seemed puzzled at my objecting to his retreat to a cell in Wandsworth.

'I know you *have* to fight it,' I assured him.

'Pity we couldn't get Teddy Singleton.' Daisy stared at me, whether in admiration or irritation I couldn't be sure. 'He wouldn't have been quite so picky.'

'I'm scared of the Molloys, Mr Rumpole. That's the truth of it.'

'Perhaps you are. But pleading guilty's not the answer.'

'It's the only answer I've got.'

'No, it isn't,' I told him. Then I had an idea. 'If you won't listen to me, perhaps I might have a word with your family. They looked a fairly sensible lot.'

*　　　*　　　*

They were all assembled in the canteen. Harry Timson, then the head of the clan, was there with his wife, Brenda, a spreading grandmother with bright, beady eyes. The much younger Fred, who was in line to succeed his father as the top Timson, was there with his warm-hearted wife, Vi, whom I was to defend on many a shoplifting charge in the future. There was Fred's brother Dennis, an expert on forged log books and 'clocking cars', as I was to discover in the years to come, and Dennis's wife, Doris, with a glamorous and heavy-lidded expression, a tight sweater and enough perfume to drown a small furry animal. It was Doris who, much later, I had to defend in a difficult case concerning the receiving of a large quantity of frozen shellfish, luxury goods as befitted Doris: langoustines, scampi, crayfish and the like.

I was only a white wig, taking on a Timson brief at the last moment, but I have to say I have never been listened to with as much courteous attention by any of the judges who deal in crime as I received from the Timson family.

For a while the evidence called concerned the Molloys, their tyrannical behaviour and desire to impose a reign of terror on south Brixton. The evidence was clear, uncontested and all one way. After twenty minutes, and the consumption of another coffee, bun and butter, I decided it was time I made my final speech. Accordingly, I tapped my coffee cup with a teaspoon and went straight to what seemed to me to be the heart of the matter.

'May it please you, members of the Timson family,' I began in a low, conversational tone, 'what Cyril is asking for is an ignominious surrender to the forces of evil. I'm sure I don't need to remind you, it's only a few years since we emerged victorious from a war with a ruthless enemy with whom I'm sure the Molloys would have had much in common. Did we quietly surrender to the Wehrmacht and to the SS? Did we say politely, "It's all our fault, so please walk over us with your storm troopers and your jackboots?"' At this point I distinctly heard Doris ask her husband what jackboots were, as though they might be some sort of fashion accessory. 'We did not! We fought back and told the truth and, in the end, we won! And if we hadn't, I ask you, what would have happened? The world would have been ruled by the Nazis.' As I was in a Churchillian mood I pronounced the word Narzeez, as he did. 'So, if we turn tail and run from the Molloys now, they'll rule Brixton, doing what they like, bearing false witness and making accusations whenever it suits them.'

'We don't want that.' Fred Timson gave me an encouraging mutter.

Then I embarked on a peroration, borrowed, I have to confess, from our wartime leader. 'We must

58

fight them in Coldharbour Lane, we must fight them on Streatham Hill and we must fight them in Clapham. We must never surrender!' And after a suitable pause I added, in what I hoped were quieter but even more persuasive tones, 'And your Uncle Cyril must never give aid and comfort to the enemy by pleading guilty just because he's frightened of the Molloys. And if you want time to discuss this among yourselves, I will step over to the slot machine and buy myself a small bar of Cadbury's milk chocolate.'

I had hardly persuaded the machine to deliver up the goods before I was called back to the table by Fred Timson. It seemed they had a verdict; but first they had a question.

'If Cyril does a "not guilty", Mr Rumpole, will you be here to defend him?'

'While I can stand on my hind legs,' I assured him, 'and while I can still speak, I will defend Uncle Cyril to the death.'

'Then he'll do a "not guilty". That's what we've all decided and Uncle Cyril was never one to give any trouble to the family.'

*   *   *

The London Sessions judge, a small foxy-faced individual known as 'Custodial Cookson' because of his lengthy sentences, was not best pleased at Uncle Cyril's apparent change of heart.

'This case was listed as a plea of guilty, Mr Rumpole. Now another date will have to be fixed for the trial. Your client is causing a good deal of trouble with the lists.'

'Any amount of trouble with the lists,' I felt

59

entitled to say, 'is less important than Mr Timson's right to a fair hearing.'

'You are of quite recent call to the bar, I think, Mr Rumpole.' 'Custodial Cookson' had a voice like dead twigs blown over a frosty window. 'Perhaps in the future you will be able to control your clients' inconvenient changes of mind.'

'I hope not, Your Honour.'

The custodial judge looked as though he would have liked to say a good deal more. Instead he told me we'd be informed of the new date and refused bail. So Uncle Cyril was remanded, for a while at least, within the safety of the prison walls.

As we crossed Blackfriars Bridge on the way back to Daisy's office and my chambers, she said, 'You did well there, didn't you, Horace?'

'You mean I upheld the finest traditions of the bar?'

'No, I mean you won yourself another brief.'

8

Back at my desk, having committed my recollections of the first of many Timson defences to the pages of these memoirs, I was once again interrupted by the voices of the present day. Claude Erskine-Brown entered without knocking, flopped himself down in my client's chair and gave a heavy and, I thought, somewhat self-satisfied sigh.

'It seems,' he said, 'that I've done it again, Rumpole.'

'I know you have. And got into deep trouble with the sisterhood of the bar.'

'It's not them I'm worried about, Rumpole. They've got nothing to complain about. Not now.'

'So what can ail thee, Erskine-Brown, alone and palely loitering?' I suppose I might have said that, but I kept quiet, hoping that the man would leave me sooner. He was, however, determined to tell me what ailed him.

'Have you broken anyone's heart, Rumpole?'

'No,' I had to confess, 'I've had rather a poor record in the heart-breaking department.'

'It happens to me all too often. People fall in love with me and of course, having regard to my present situation, it can never be.'

'What can never be?'

'What they all want.'

'And what is that exactly?'

'I suppose,' Erskine-Brown said in all modesty, 'me.'

'And you think you've broken a heart?'

61

Now Claude gave vent to a heavy sigh and tried to sound suitably regretful. 'It's the effect I seem to have on people.'

'Is it really? I don't think you've broken my heart yet, Erskine-Brown.'

'Of course not, Rumpole. Your heart's probably reinforced concrete for all I know. I'm speaking now of younger women.'

'Do you have one particular younger woman in mind?'

'Haven't I told you? It's Lala Ingolsby. Probert's pupil.'

'And what are the precise symptoms of her heart trouble?'

'You won't spread this around chambers, will you, Rumpole? It's not the sort of story one wants to have repeated in the clerk's room.' Claude struck a cautionary note.

'My lips will be sealed. In perpetuity.'

'Well, then, of course she's fallen head over heels—'

'A nasty accident?' I hadn't really misunderstood him.

'No, in love. She wanted us to be together—for always.'

'A long time,' I agreed.

'What's more, *she* wanted to ring up Philly and tell her we wanted a divorce. I had to put a stop to it, Rumpole. You do see that, don't you?'

'Embarrassment all round, I suppose.'

'I'm glad you agree. I mean, you simply don't get a divorce from your wife if that wife is a High Court judge. Besides which, there are the children to consider.'

'Tristan and Isolde?' I knew their operatically

inspired names, having taken them to the pantomime.

'One simply can't wreck their faith in family life.'

'I suppose that's on your mind all the time?'

'Of course it is. That's why I had to tell the poor girl—'

'Lala?'

'Probert's pupil. It can never be.'

'And when she heard that she went, I suppose, into a decline, took a long holiday in Thailand, joined the French Foreign Legion?'

'She's being incredibly brave about it, Rumpole. She turned up for work just as though nothing had happened.'

'And you made no reference whatever to the shape of her legs?'

'Never again, Rumpole, those days are over. Never again.'

To the accompaniment of another heavy sigh, I took up my pen again to attack these memoirs. When I next looked up, Erskine-Brown had palely loitered out of the room.

* * *

After the visit to London Sessions and my speech designed to stiffen the sinews and summon up the blood of the Timson family in their fight against the tyranny of the Molloys, I felt a vague pang of regret that I hadn't ended the speech in question with a cry of 'God for Rumpole! England and Saint George!' After all that excitement, time seemed to stand still.

So I was alone in Uncle Tom's room, long after he'd gone home. I was gazing once again at the

63

photographs of the scene of the crime, what my old law tutor at Keble, Septimus Porter, had taught me to call the *'locus in quo'*. For what seemed to me like the hundredth time, I was staring at the dead pilot officer slumped in his armchair with a half-open door behind him. I was wondering whether to go for a chop in the Charing Cross Lyon's Corner House before returning to my lonely bedsit off Southampton Row when a question occurred to me which called, as I thought, for an immediate answer. Accordingly, I put a call through to the offices of our Penge solicitors.

'I'm afraid Mr Barnsley Gough has had to leave. Can I help you at all, Mr Rumpole?' It was the voice of the eager young man, hardly more than a boy, who, I remembered, knew most about the case.

'Is that Bernard?'

'Yes, Mr Rumpole.'

'Hail, Bonny Bernard.' I have no idea why I called him that, but it's a name which has stuck to him over the years during which, apart from a few moments of regrettable infidelity, he has been my perpetual support. 'It has occurred to me that I would like to take a look at the *locus.*'

'He's in it.'

'What?'

'Our client is in the lock—whatever you said.'

'No, Bonny Bernard. The *"locus in quo"*. The scene of the crime. Can we see it?'

'I don't know . . .'

'It'll be perfectly simple. You'll just have to fix it with the officer in charge of the case. And tell the prosecution, they're entitled to be there.'

'And your leader, Mr Rumpole?'

'Oh, I'll tell Mr Wystan all about it, of course.'

'All right, then. I'll let Albert know what I've fixed up. You got an idea, have you?'

'An idea? I might just have a few more questions to ask.'

'Tell me, Mr Rumpole.' Bonny Bernard still sounded keen.

'Simon told us there was one man at the party who tried to stop them attacking him. Fellow named Harry . . .'

'Harry Daniels?' Bernard remembered.

'He's not on the list of prosecution witnesses. Get in touch with him, would you? He might give evidence for us.'

'You think it's worth trying?'

'I think everything's worth trying. In this particular case.'

*   *   *

It looked dusty and neglected, as though a feeling of guilt, the result of a violent death, still hung about it, and for which the room itself took some sort of blame. I had met Bonny Bernard at the bus stop and we had walked through the sifting rain to the row of identical bungalows in a dead-end street behind Penge Road. There was a police car parked outside number 3, the home of the Jerolds. We were met by Detective Superintendent Spalding, the officer in charge of the case. He was the sort of straight-backed, poker-up-the-backside, pursed-lipped policeman who clearly regarded our visit as a waste of his and everybody else's time. He was also not the kind of officer I could imagine collecting odd scraps of information from the

Timsons in the Needle Arms.

So we stood in the room, which seemed small to have accommodated a party of half-drunk wartime heroes and a sudden tragedy. The bungalows were identical so 'Tail-End' Charlie had precisely the same accommodation as his pilot officer. Jerry's front door opened on to a small hall, not much more than a short passage with another door opening into the sitting room, from where a door led to another passage with access to two bedrooms, a kitchen and the bathroom. There was a back door to an area where the dustbin stood in which the Luger pistol was eventually found.

Such garden as there was, a pocket handkerchief of dark earth containing a few straggling roses and dahlias, was crossed by a crazy-paving pathway from the gate to the front door. It seemed a meagre place to come home to after the daring splendours of a victorious war.

The trophies of that war seemed diminished and almost irrelevant after the most recent violent crime that had taken place in the room. The photographs of Pilot Officer Jerry looked curled and untidy on the mantelpiece, his silk scarf was crumpled and the pride of the collection, the captured German pistol, had already been tested for fingerprints, wrapped in cellophane and labelled Prosecution Exhibit One.

The armchair was about six feet away from the artificial coals in the electric fire. It wasn't facing the fireplace but turned away at an angle, so Jerry Jerold had not died looking directly at the relics of his past. On the floor beside his chair, an almost empty bottle of Famous Grouse whisky had been found, on which there were fingerprints of the

66

party of ex-RAF men, including Jerry. There was also a half-empty soda water siphon and an empty glass with only Jerry's fingerprints on it.

At one point, when the gloomy superintendent was off with his attendant detective sergeant in the kitchen, I invited Bonny Bernard to sit in the armchair. I stood over him pointing an imaginary gun, at which dramatic moment the officer in charge of the case returned to utter a sad rebuke.

'Mr Rumpole, I know you're young in call to the bar but I don't believe Mr Wystan, had he been here, would have asked his instructing solicitor to sit down upon the exhibits.'

At which Bonny Bernard climbed to his feet, looking embarrassed, and I gave my attention to other matters. It was about three yards from the chair to the door into the hallway and the same distance to the front door. The position of the bloodstains had been circled in chalk and I was on my knees examining them when I heard the all too familiar voice of Reggie Proudfoot braying in the air above me.

'Doing a bit of detective work, are you, Sherlock Rumpole?'

'As a matter of fact, yes.' I did my best to silence this legal pain in the backside. 'And it so happens that we've got a cast-iron defence. What are you doing here?'

'Same as you, Rumpole. I'm a junior, but I've got the good luck to be one of the juniors for the prosecution, which means that, unlike you, I'm on a winner.'

'Are you sure of that?'

'Of course I'm sure. You're going to lose your case, just as you lost your dancing partner.'

67

'I really don't see the connection,' I suppose I made the mistake of showing my anger, 'between a hop in the Inner Temple and a young boy on trial for his life.'

'Don't you, Rumpole? You're the connection. You're a loser in both places.' It was then he looked round the accommodation, not to search for any hint of a clue but merely to make a general observation. 'My God, it must be ghastly living in a bungalow. No wonder it led to murder!'

I left the scene of the crime with Bonny Bernard. When he asked me if I thought our visit had been at all helpful, I said possibly, and then thought that we'd been concentrating on the death of Jerry Jerold and seemed to forget the other murder. What did we know about 'Tail-End' Charlie? He was found dead by the cleaning lady. Was he married? What about girlfriends? He must have been alone on the night he was shot. I asked Bonny Bernard, 'Will you find out?'

'Will I do it? Of course I'll do it. I can't leave that sort of thing to Mr Barnsley Gough.' Then young Bernard gave me a small conspiratorial smile. 'He's fully occupied with his golf!'

*   *   *

'I can understand, Rumpole, how your connection with an important case has led you astray. It has caused you to make an error of judgement.'

'I just thought you were probably too busy to visit the scene of the crime.'

'No, you didn't think I was too busy.' C. H. Wystan was in a surprisingly serene, even a forgiving, mood. 'You wanted to do something on your own. Of course I understand that. The feeling was perfectly natural. And I'm sure it won't happen again.'

'Of course not,' I assured him. I had got what I wanted from the Penge bungalow.

'That's understood, then. I don't suppose your visit did us any harm. Or our client any particular good.'

'You've read my notes?' I had written down my thoughts about, among other things, the position of the armchair.

'Of course I've read your notes, dear boy.' It was the first time, positively the first time, that Hilda's father had called me his 'dear boy' and the fact left me, I have to confess, gulping as he went on, 'But there is one unfortunate fact that you seem to have overlooked. One question I would suggest that, for all your industry, you've failed to ask. If young Jerold didn't shoot his father, or the person apparently known as "Tail-End" Charlie, then who on earth did?'

9

A few days later, I got a call from Bonny Bernard, who said he'd found Harry Daniels's address and had spoken to him on the telephone.

'Can he help us?'

'I'm not quite sure. He said he hoped young Simon would get off. And he said Jerry Jerold probably deserved what he got.'

'Did he mean for taunting his son?'

'I'm not sure.'

'I suppose he might have meant that. Did he say anything else?'

'Not then. But I've made a date to call on him and take a statement.'

'Oh, well done, Bonny Bernard, well done indeed! And Charlie Weston?'

'Simon gave me some more information. He had a wife, Katie, but it was an eventful kind of marriage.'

'How do you mean "eventful"?'

'Well, apparently the violence was mutual. Charlie sometimes appeared with a face covered in scratches and once a black eye.'

'Katie took a swing at him?'

'Something like that. Anyway, they'd split up for the umpteenth time a month before the night at the Palladium.'

I thanked the industrious Bernard again and rang off. In all probability, Daniels's evidence would do nothing to answer C. H. Wystan's question. But it was encouraging to find someone who seemed to be on our side. For the next few days, as I waited for a new witness statement, I lived in a condition of vague hope.

*   *   *

It was while I was waiting for further news from this front that I got more words of warning from our clerk, Albert Handyside, in Pommeroy's Wine Bar.

'The duty of the leader is to lead, Mr Rumpole. It's for him to decide what witnesses to call and the general conduct of the case. It's the duty of the junior—'

'I know,' I told Albert, 'it's the junior's duty to take a full note of the evidence. And occasionally buy his leader a cup of coffee.'

'You've got it, Mr Rumpole! Got it in one!' Albert smiled and dipped his head towards the pint of Guinness I'd bought him. Encouraged by the investigation undertaken by Bonny Bernard and my good self, I took a swig of my glass of Château Fleet Street. Then I asked, 'But if the junior has a few ideas that might help the leader to win the case?'

'It's not the junior's job to have ideas, Mr Rumpole. In my opinion, you can count yourself extremely lucky to have a junior brief in an important matter. You have to be content with taking a note. Or calling a short and unimportant witness if your leader invites you to do so.'

'And did my leader invite you to have a word with me on this subject?'

'Mr C. H. Wystan, QC, your leader and Head of Chambers, thought it might sound better coming from me, seeing as we take the occasional drink together and I've put a bit of work in your direction.'

At this I heard a scarcely suppressed giggle and, for the first time, I noticed that the abominable Reggie Proudfoot had come into the bar with the junior clerk from the DPP's office I had seen with him in the fatal bungalow. The man had certainly been earwigging our conversation. Before I could attend to Proudfoot, or indeed to Albert's lecture on the proprieties of the legal profession, I saw the fresh face of young Bonny Bernard making its way through the crowded Pommeroy's.

'They said in the clerk's room you'd both be in here,' he said when he arrived. 'I was up in the City and I thought I'd tell you about Harry Daniels.'

'You've been at it again, haven't you, Mr Rumpole?' Albert spoke sadly.

'Yes, of course.' I turned to Bonny Bernard. 'The man who said Simon's father deserved all he got. Have you taken a statement?'

'The man's done the vanishing trick, Mr Rumpole.' Bernard was apologetic. 'He wasn't there when I went round to take his statement. The house was all locked up. Gone away with no word when he'd be back—that's what a neighbour told me. I'm sorry it's a disappointment for you.'

'Does Mr Wystan know that you've been making enquiries?' interrupted Albert.

Bernard looked blank, so I had to answer Albert's question. 'Not yet. But when we get some results he'll be the first to know.'

'I'm still trying to get the details of the other witnesses,' Bernard went on brightly, causing deeper looks of disapproval from Albert. 'They're being a bit slow at RAF records.'

73

'It doesn't appear—' Albert seemed relieved at the thought—'that all your research is having much of a result.'

'Not yet perhaps,' I told him. 'I thought of going away this weekend, up to see friends I met in the RAF. They keep the Crooked Billet at Coldsands-on-Sea.'

'Have you told Mr Wystan that?'

'Not yet. I promise you I'll let him know if I learn anything useful.'

Albert gave me a sour look and drained his glass of Guinness. 'I told Mr Wystan I'd have a word with you and I've done it. So I hope you'll bear what I've said in mind.'

'I shall, Albert. Of course I shall. You've got the wisdom of generations of clerks who've told young white wigs how to behave. I know that. There's only one thing more important than keeping my leader happy.'

'What's that, then?'

'Trying to save young Simon's life.'

'I only hope, Mr Rumpole—' Albert put his empty glass down on the bar—'that you're as clever as you think you are.' With that he left us, and Bernard and I moved to a table in Pommeroy's, as we were to do so often in the years to come, for further discussions. As we went, I saw out of the corner of my eye the young DPP clerk with Reggie Proudfoot scribble a note on the front page of his *Evening Standard*.

*   *   *

When I chronicled those I had been in love with, it was, I'm afraid, only a small number and, to some

74

of my readers perhaps, an unimpressive list. I never aspired to the adventures of Casanova or the 1,003 conquests made by Don Giovanni in Italy alone. However, those I have named had, each of them, a deep effect on me and it was to one of their number my thoughts turned when I tried, in vain, to answer the searching and vital question posed me by my not particularly learned leader, C. H. Wystan. 'If Simon Jerold didn't shoot his father, then who the hell did?'

I had read and re-read all the prosecution statements so that I knew them by heart when I got out of the train, one Saturday afternoon, at Coldsands-on-Sea. A wind swept this seaside resort on the Norfolk coast, home to the old RAF station where I had served, however unheroically, as ground staff during the recent conflict.

The saloon bar of the Crooked Billet had this much in common with the living room at number 3 Paxton Street, Penge: it was a kind of museum of tributes to the war in the air. There was no gun, no bullets, but a captured Nazi helmet, a plaster image of Winston Churchill which could actually hold up two fingers in a 'V' sign and puff smoke out of a cigar, a signed photograph of Vera Lynn and a model of a Spitfire swinging from the ceiling. Even the pintable reminded me of an antique looted from the NAAFI of my old station. All of this was familiar enough, but my heart beat a little faster when the person who had been bent double, putting away bottles on the shelves behind the bar, straightened up and greeted me with her never-forgotten smile.

She was no longer in the uniform of a WAAF. She was wearing a frilly shirt and dark blue trousers. And then, only seven years since her demob, the years had not added much to the generosity of her curves or dimmed the brightness of her hair. Bobby Dougherty looked much as she had when she was Bobby O'Keefe, before her heart was stolen away by Pilot Officer Sam 'Three Fingers' Dougherty, who was without doubt a wartime hero and so had attractions with which a mere member of the ground staff could never compete. But now we were alone together and she was smiling, surrounded by the fairy lights along the bar and the comforting smell of stale booze, getting ready for opening time.

'Hello, darling!' Bobby gave me a breathless kiss which decorated my cheek with lipstick. 'Long time no see. I've missed you.' I was complacent enough to let myself believe she was telling the truth.

That evening, after the bar closed, we three were at the pub piano. Bobby picked out the old tunes and vamped the accompaniments to 'Somewhere in France with You', 'We're Going to Hang out the Washing on the Siegfried Line', 'There'll be Bluebirds over the White Cliffs of Dover', 'You are My Sunshine' and 'Roll out the Barrel'.

Ex-Pilot Officer Sam Dougherty had appeared early in the evening. My successful rival in love was, I have to admit, a tall good-looking man wearing an RAF scarf tucked into an open-necked shirt, a blazer and scuffed suede shoes. The years had not been so kind to him as they had to Bobby. His dark hair and moustache were peppered with grey and I noticed his three fingers had trembled a little as he filled and then refreshed his glass of whisky.

Singing wartime songs, calling up wartime memories, running the bar and eating bacon and

76

eggs around midnight left little time and I went to bed with my intended questions unanswered. I lay awake for a while, listening to the murmur of the sea and trying not to think of Bobby in bed with her three-fingered husband.

It was not until Sunday morning that I suggested to Sam a 'constitutional'. This meant a brisk walk by the grey, heaving sea in the teeth of a minor gale which might, for all I knew, have been blowing from the steppes of Russia across the flat north of Europe to send teeth chattering in Coldsands-on-Sea. It was in these adverse weather conditions that I broached my subject.

'Bristol bombers.' I threw the words into the wind. 'That's what he was flying.'

'Fairly short-range,' Sam told me. 'They went after arms depots, factories, fighter stations in northern France.'

'So the crew was . . .'

'Pilot officer—'

'That was Jerry Jerold.'

'Rear gunner—'

' "Tail-End" Charlie.'

'And a navigator of course.'

'Of course. I'd forgotten about the navigator.'

'They wouldn't get very far without him.'

'I suppose they wouldn't. That's three. Did they always fly together? I didn't get to know a lot about bombers.'

'Yes. The chaps I knew in Bristols always went out with the same team. So long as they stayed alive.'

'And that wasn't necessarily very long?'

'As I remember, they were pretty good aims with anti-aircraft guns in northern France. And German

77

fighters of course.'

'Jerry Jerold and "Tail-End" Charlie were lucky to survive?'

'We were all lucky.' Sam Dougherty had stopped for a cigarette, sheltering his flickering lighter from the wind with his cupped hand. 'Unbelievably lucky.'

'And you fought on to the end of the war?'

'To the very last day of it. You know that, Rumpole.'

'Jerry and Charlie missed quite a lot of it. According to Simon, their plane was brought down.'

'They were prisoners—all three of them?'

'I suppose so.'

'So they were all lucky.'

'Not really. Not Jerry and Charlie.'

'But they survived the war.'

'Oh, yes. They survived the war all right. It was the peace that killed them. The point is, Sam, I don't feel I know enough about them. I'm defending Jerry's son, who's meant to have killed them both.'

'I know, I read about it. Bloody awful business.'

'Is there anyone you know in Bristol bombers, anyone who could tell us a bit more, anyone who might have known them? Or knew more about their story?'

Sam didn't answer me. Instead he sounded appalled. 'You're actually defending that boy?'

'Yes, Sam. I'm actually defending him.'

'Why on earth are you doing that?'

'Because he tells me he didn't do it. Because it's my job. Mainly because I want to avoid another death. Please, Sam, if you can think of anyone who might remember . . .'

'I'm a bit out of touch with the old crowd now. Living in the pub and all that. But I suppose I could ask around.'

'Oh, yes.' I did my best to sound encouraging. 'Please ask around.'

We were further along the shoreline, sliding on the wet pebbles which gave Coldsands an uncomfortable beach. A golden retriever was lifting its leg to pee in the edge of the foam that clawed at the shingle. Its owner, a grey-haired woman in a flapping mackintosh, stood calling the dog and waving a lead, but her cries were blown away on the wind. I asked 'Three Fingers' if the operations over northern France were particularly scaring.

'Scaring? Of course, we were all scared. Every single day, scared almost to death.'

'Almost, but not quite?'

'Every bloody day,' Sam confessed, 'I thought it'd be my last. You saw how horribly easy it was when you scored a direct hit. The plane buzzing around burst into flames. That's the way I'll go, you told yourself. In a bloody great ball of fire dropping out of the sky.'

We had reached a refuge, a glassed-in bus shelter on the sea front, when he said, 'And if it didn't happen one day, you were damn sure you'd buy it the next, or the next after that. You got a feeling you'd do anything to stop it.'

'Anything?'

'Well, anything within reason.'

'What would that entail?'

'I don't know. I just couldn't think. I suppose that's why I went on doing it.'

'And you survived. And now you're happily married.' I tried to keep the note of envy out of

79

my voice.

'I suppose I am,' he conceded with, I thought, a surprising reluctance. 'Bobby's a good girl. She doesn't nag me about the amount of whisky I get through. She's not like my bloody doctor. Well, I told him I have to drink enough to go to sleep without dreaming.'

I watched the raindrops chasing each other down the glass of the shelter. At the end of our bench an elderly tramp was muttering as he unwrapped a sandwich from a sheet of newspaper. Which war, I wondered, did he dream about?

'You had bad dreams, then?' I asked 'Three Fingers' Sam.

'Still have them. About catching on fire and falling out of the bloody sky. Sometimes you wondered what the point of it all was. People killing each other. We never said that of course.'

'No, we never said it.'

'There was a bloke used to go into one of the pubs we went to. He was in some sort of reserved occupation connected to the Ministry of Food or something. He was always saying there wasn't any point in going on with the war and Hitler had some of the right ideas anyway.'

'You never agreed with that?'

'No. We just laughed at him. I think someone once beat him up. Did you lose your faith in the war, Rumpole?'

'Oh, I was in the ground staff.'

' "Grounded Rumpole".'

'Perhaps that made it easier to stay patriotic.'

'Anyway, it's all over now.'

Not quite over, I thought, in the Penge bungalows.

I said goodbye to Sam after the bar closed on Sunday afternoon. He was standing under the fairy lights, contemplating a solitary whisky. 'Bobby,' he told me, 'has gone upstairs to have a kip. She asked me to say her goodbyes.'

'Well, then,' I said, 'goodbye.'

'You didn't come to ask me all these questions, did you, Rumpole? You came up here to see her.'

'Partly,' I had to admit.

'Partly?' He sounded doubtful. 'Perhaps she ought to have married you. Barrister at law might have made a better husband than pub keeper on the sauce.'

'She loved you,' I told him.

'Was it me? Was it the wings on the uniform and every day going out to die. I had that advantage over you, Rumpole. You were always down on the ground, weren't you, and likely to stay alive.'

So, accepting the situation as one of the inevitable results of the war, I left Coldsands without the goodbye kiss I had, no doubt foolishly, looked forward to.

On the slow train back to London, I re-read the prosecution statements of all the ex-airmen who had been at the reunion. None of them claimed to have been the navigator who flew with Pilot Officer Jerry and 'Tail-End' Charlie, nor was there any indication of who he might have been. I decided to ask Bonny Bernard to make further enquiries.

10

'Mr Rochford, you live over the shop Sound Universe in Coldharbour Lane?'

I had felt the usual courtroom terrors of a white wig: sweaty hands, dry mouth and a strong temptation to run out of the door and take up work as a quietly unostentatious bus conductor or lavatory attendant. But once I had asked the first question in my cross-examination of the chief prosecution witness in Uncle Cyril's case, my head cleared, my hands no longer sweated and a possibly misleading confidence came over me.

'Me and my wife live there, yes,' the shop owner answered my question.

The man from whom Uncle Cyril was alleged to have stolen radios and an egg-timer was tall and scrawny with glasses and a look of perpetual anxiety. And there was I, in my rather too white wig and much too new gown, cross-examining with my guns blazing, uncomfortably aware that I might be shot down in a ball of fire at any minute by 'Custodial Cookson', the not so learned judge at London Sessions, who knew that Uncle Cyril had once been prepared to plead guilty and obviously took the view that this trial was a completely unnecessary waste of time for all concerned.

Behind me were the troops I had persuaded to follow me into battle, the Timson family, after I had made my stirring speech in the canteen. In the dock, Uncle Cyril was smiling in a detached sort of way, as though the proceedings were really nothing much to do with him. On the bench beside me sat the prosecutor, Vincent Caraway, an elderly junior with a grey moustache and a voice which seemed about to fade away in terminal boredom. He was reading his brief in another case, convinced that Uncle Cyril would be sent back to prison without any particular effort on his part being necessary.

Three scowling men sat in the front row of the public gallery, sending distinct messages of ill-will towards me as I conducted one of my earliest cross-examinations. The eldest, the Timsons told me, was 'Nighty', the undisputed leader of the rival clan, celebrated for saying 'Nighty-night' to those who frustrated his plans and who weren't, in some cases, expected to survive until the following morning.

'So perhaps you'd like to tell us this, Mr Rochford, what time did you and your wife go to bed the night that Cyril Timson is alleged to have broken into your shop?'

'Mr Rumpole,' 'Custodial Cookson' was clearly losing whatever patience he had, 'could you confine your cross-examination to relevant matters, or are you going to enquire at what time Mr and Mrs Rochford drank their final cup of Horlicks?' His Custodial Honour got what I felt was a cheap laugh from the jury with this Horlicks line. I tried to sound serious and judicial as a contrast to the jokey judge, although I was probably too young for it.

'I think,' I said, 'the jury may be interested in the suggestion that Mr and Mrs Rochford slept throughout this alleged break-in.'

'Mr Rumpole! What do you mean by the word "alleged"? Are you suggesting there wasn't a break-in?'

'If Your Honour will allow me to continue with my questions, the court will discover exactly what I

84

am suggesting.' It was the first time I had been in the least bit rude, even to a mere London Sessions judge, and the effect of it was like that on a young girl who takes her first gulp of champagne. I'm afraid it went to my head. 'Yes, Mr Rochford,' I went on before 'Custodial Cookson' had time to interrupt again, 'I think what this jury will want to know is what time you think you went to sleep, after, as His Honour said, you had your Horlicks and read your books?'

'Books!' Mr Rochford looked at me with increased suspicion, as though I had suggested some bizarre form of sexual activity. 'We do not read books. We work hard, Mr Rumpole. In Sound Universe.'

'I'm sure you do. So may we assume you were asleep by midnight?'

'Certainly by midnight.'

'And you didn't wake up until about two a.m., when you went to the window and you say you saw my client, Cyril Timson, loading a television set into the back of a white van?'

'That's right,' the witness was helpful enough to admit.

'Mr Rumpole,' His Custodial Honour was restive again, 'he has told us he was woken by sounds in the shop below.'

'Quite right.' I attempted the reply aloof. 'But that could only have been the last article, the television being removed from the shop. Is that right?'

'It must have been.' Mr Rochford was thinking it over.

'So someone broke open the shop door, disconnected your rather primitive burglar alarm

85

and moved a number of radios out to a van without waking you or Mrs Rochford?'

'So it would seem.'

'A deep sleep!'

'The wife and I are good sleepers.'

'After perhaps a slug of whisky in the Horlicks?' It wasn't worth calling a joke, but it earned a laugh from the jury and a sharp reprimand from 'Custodial Cookson'.

'Mr Rumpole, you must learn that London Sessions is not a theatre! We're not a place of entertainment! Your client is facing a serious charge and you would do well to take it seriously.' It was not the last time I was to be accused of making jokes in court, and, I flatter myself, the jokes got better as the years went by. Jokes in court, I have discovered, usually side with the defence.

'Very well,' I said. 'In deference to His Honour's wishes, let me ask you a serious question. Do you know a Mr Terry Molloy?'

It was a question which seemed to cause the witness some difficulty. He was silent for a while and then said, with considerable reluctance, 'I might do.'

'I should think you might just possibly have heard of him. Isn't he your landlord?' Daisy Sampson, for all her red lips and seductive ways, had done her research well. The owner of the Sound Universe premises was Terry; it was only a part, Daisy had discovered, of his considerable investment in property around the south Brixton area.

'I can't see that it matters in the least who's the landlord of the premises your client is said to have

86

broken into. Mr Caraway, do you object to this line of questioning?'

'Custodial Cookson' called for reinforcements. However, the experienced Vincent Caraway rose languidly to his feet as though it was really too much trouble to interrupt the childish performance of a white wig. 'No objection, Your Honour. If my learned friend is allowed to continue, we may discover what point he is attempting to make.'

'That's extremely generous of you, Mr Caraway.' The custodial one was wreathed in smiles as he addressed one of London Sessions' regulars. The smile died as he said, 'Mr Rumpole, Mr Caraway has, in his generosity, decided not to object to your line of questioning. You may deal with it shortly. So far as I can see it has little relevance to this case.'

'There is someone who does find it relevant to this case, though, isn't there, Mr Rochford?' I thought it better to engage with the witness rather than prolonging a somewhat fruitless argument with His Honour. 'Isn't your landlord here in court, in the front row of the public gallery?'

'I can't see him.' Mr Rochford was looking everywhere except in the direction of the Molloys.

'Just look up at the public gallery. Do you not see Mr Terence, also known as "Nighty", Molloy?'

'Mr Molloy?'

'Yes. He's here, isn't he?'

'Maybe he is.'

'If he owns the premises,' 'Custodial Cookson' was anxious to help the witness, 'quite naturally he's interested in the result of this trial. Have you any more *relevant* questions, Mr Rumpole?'

'Just a few, Your Honour. Mr Rochford, you say you looked out of the window and saw my client,

Cyril Timson, putting the television set into a white van.'

'Yes, I saw him.'

'It was two a.m. and presumably dark?'

'He was stood under a street lamp.'

'Oh, was he really? How very thoughtful of him! No doubt he was anxious to be recognized.'

I got a small laugh from the jury for this and a further reminder from His Honour that we were not in a theatre.

'And are you telling this jury,' I was determined to go on, whether or not the judge thought I was taking part in a theatrical event, 'you were able to pick out Cyril Timson at an identity parade after the brief glance at him from a window at two in the morning?'

'It wasn't just that.' Mr Rochford sounded shocked at my suggestion. 'I'd seen the photograph, hadn't I?'

'What photograph was that?' I pricked up my ears. I decided to put the next question in a way that might appeal even to our judge. 'Are you suggesting that Detective Inspector White, the very experienced officer in charge of the case, showed you a photograph of his suspect *before* you attended the identity parade?'

'He might have done.'

'He'll be giving evidence and I'll have to put it to him. I'm sure his answer will be it would have been grossly improper of the police to do any such thing.'

'All right, then.' The witness saw danger ahead and started to retreat. 'Someone showed me a photograph of Timson.'

'Someone? Can't you remember who it was?'

88

'I can't exactly remember.'

'Then let me make a suggestion which might jog your memory. Was it perhaps Mr Terence "Nighty" Molloy?'

The manager of Sound Universe looked up at the public gallery then as though for help but, getting none, he was driven to mutter, 'No, I don't *think* so.'

'You don't *think* so?' I gave the jury the look of someone who has scored a direct hit, gathered my gown about me and sat down in a triumphant sort of way. The judge did his best to restore the fortunes of the prosecution and to wipe the smile off my face.

'Mr Rochford, you don't think it was this Mr Molloy who showed you the photograph? Are you not sure of that?'

'Oh, yes.' The witness looked considerably relieved. 'I think I'm sure.' And although the judge wrote this answer down with apparent satisfaction, it seemed to leave us more or less where we were before.

*   *   *

The trial wound its slow way onwards. Among the last of the prosecution witnesses, Detective Inspector 'Persil' White gave us the pleasure of his company. He seemed a perfectly reasonable police officer and I thought he might be willing to help us. I hadn't reckoned on the enthusiasm with which 'Custodial Cookson' was prepared to help the prosecution out of the lazy and somewhat careless hands of the experienced Vincent Caraway.

'Detective Inspector, do you from time to time

frequent a local pub known as the Needle Arms?' I asked.

'I take a drink there occasionally.'

'And do you sometimes pick up helpful information about local crimes and who commits them?'

'Let's say I learn more about crime in Britain at the Needle Arms than I would if I stopped at home reading the paper.'

'And did you get the information about the Sound Universe break-in from someone in the Needle Arms?'

'I might have done.' 'Persil' was becoming cautious.

'And was that someone a member of the Molloy family?'

'Mr Rumpole,' the custodial expression had been screwed back on the judge's face, 'are you intending to call this member of the Molloy family as a witness?'

The answer was that I thought any member of the Molloy family would be as likely to help the defence as Judge Cookson was to place Uncle Cyril, if found guilty, upon probation. So I told him, 'No, Your Honour, I am not calling any member of the Molloy family.'

'Then I suppose, Mr Caraway, the nature of your objection would be that any communication between the officer and this person from the Molloy family would be pure hearsay.'

He had managed to catch the attention of our prosecutor, otherwise engaged in reading his brief in another case. So the experienced, languid Caraway stood up, murmured, 'Your Honour puts it so much better than I could,' and sank back into his seat.

'So there you are, Mr Rumpole! May I say that I entirely agree with Mr Caraway's cogent argument. Let's have no mention of this officer's conversation with any Molloy.'

'Very well, Your Honour. Then let me ask you this, Detective Inspector. Did my client, Cyril Timson, say to you that he bet the Molloys accused him of the Sound Universe job because he'd fingered Jimmy Molloy for the Meadowsweet break-in? And before there is any objection to that, may I make it clear that I will be calling my client, and so what he said certainly isn't hearsay.'

'Are you objecting, Mr Caraway?' 'Custodial Cookson' looked hopefully at the prosecution.

'Not really, Your Honour. The jury will remember that this witness has already told them that Cyril Timson admitted his guilt, and this case first came on as a mere plea in mitigation.' After this comparatively long speech, Vincent Caraway sank back in his seat, exhausted. But His Honour was delighted.

'Yes, of course he did. You will remember that, won't you, members of the jury? Mr Timson, in the dock over there, originally admitted this charge.'

And, in the end, they remembered it.

*　　*　　*

It's painful to contemplate your disasters, and as I sat alone that evening I was tempted to ask my landlady if there was any sort of opening for me in the rubber johnnie shop and give up the bar entirely.

It was no use telling myself I'd done my best,

that I'd got DI White to agree that the Molloys hated the Timsons, that I had got most of Cyril's story into evidence in the face of a hail of small-arms fire from the bench, that I'd called Uncle Cyril to explain that he'd only felt safe in prison, which was why he had pleaded guilty to an offence he didn't commit. I had carefully prepared my final speech to the jury.

'This case has only taken us a few days,' I told them. 'Soon you will be back to your normal lives and you'll have forgotten all about the radio and television shop in Coldharbour Lane and the Needle Arms and the Molloys, who we say were prepared to arrange a break-in at their own premises in order to punish old Cyril Timson, who might have informed on them. All these things are only part of your lives, and a small part at that. But for Cyril Timson, the frightened, elderly man I represent, this is one of the most important moments of his life. Can you send him to prison on this evidence, in this strange and unusual case? Members of the jury, I leave the future life of Uncle Cyril Timson in your hands, for you and not His Honour are the sole judges of the facts in this case, and I am confident that your verdict will be "Not guilty".'

This peroration was one I have since used, with a few essential adjustments, in hundreds of cases. I have always found it effective, but in *R*. v. *Timson* it failed to work the oracle.

Uncle Tom told me that, in the old days at London Sessions, the jury would merely be asked to turn to each other and, after a few whispered words, agree on a verdict. 'Custodial Cookson' at least allowed them to retire; but after half an hour

92

they were back to give Cyril what he had always said he wanted, two years safe inside.

'I'm very sorry.' I felt I could hardly bring myself to face Harry Timson. I have to say I was surprised by his reaction to the result.

'You did great, Mr Rumpole! We never had a brief who put a judge in his place the way you did. And that speech! It brought my wife, Brenda, near to tears. Let's just hope this case is the first of many you do for the Timson family.'

'But you don't seem to understand. I lost!'

'That's immaterial, that is. Old Uncle Cyril, he's happy with the result anyway. Lost you may have done, but it's the way you lost impressed us!'

*   *   *

I didn't find these words of Harry Timson, kindly meant I'm sure, any particular comfort. Back in my lonely bedsit, I struck my boiled eggs hard and viciously with the spoon. Before falling asleep, I flicked though the *Oxford Book of English Verse* (the old Arthur Quiller-Couch edition) that has been my constant companion since my schooldays, and found one of my favourite bits of Wordsworth, the Old Sheep of the Lake District.

> For this, for everything, we are out of tune;
> It moves us not.—Great God! I'd rather be
> A Pagan suckled in a creed outworn;
> So might I, standing on this pleasant lea,
> Have glimpses that would make me less forlorn;
> Have sight of Proteus rising from the sea;
> Or hear old Triton blow his wreathèd horn.

I closed my eyes. All was silent. Of old Triton blowing his wreathèd horn there was not a squeak.

*   *   *

The next day in chambers, I was still thinking about the two cases: the one I had lost and the other my leader, C. H. Wystan, was clearly prepared to lose. And then I had a telephone call from Bonny Bernard.

'Just got an answer from the RAF, Mr Rumpole. You wanted to know about the third chap in the bomber. The navigator.'

'Well, Jerry Jerold and "Tail-End" Charlie were so close, I just thought the third man in their plane might be able to tell us a bit more about them.'

'His name was David Galloway.'

'It might just be worthwhile getting a statement off him.'

'Can't be done, I'm afraid, Mr Rumpole.'

'Why ever not? The prosecution couldn't object.'

'It's not that, they've got it in the records. Galloway went missing, believed dead.'

So that doorway of enquiry was closed. But now I had every confidence in Bonny Bernard's powers of research. 'Listen carefully,' I said, as though I had masterminded a hundred murder trials. 'I want you to find out all you can about the backgrounds and war records of all the officers who were at the party that night after the theatre. Can you do that?'

'I'll do it for you, Mr Rumpole,' Bonny Bernard was quick enough to answer. 'I'll certainly do it. But will *you* ever be able to use all that information?'

'Who knows?' I did my best to encourage his

94

labours. 'In a trial like this, who knows what's going to happen?'

I said this, of course, because I still had no clear idea of what I was looking for.

11

'What are you doing, Rumpole?'

'Remembering.'

'Well try and remember with your leg elevated. You know what Dr McClintock said.'

'Dr McClintock never tried to write his memoirs with one leg cocked up on a joint stool.' I thought this a fair point to put to She Who Must Be Obeyed, although I accommodated her by raising my leg.

'What are these memoirs you're talking about, Rumpole?'

'The most important time of my life, when I did the Penge Bungalow Murders.'

'*And* when we met?'

'That too.'

'Or had you forgotten?'

'Of course not, Hilda,' I hastened to reassure her. 'You changed my life, you and the Penge Bungalow case.'

'It changed mine too, but whether it was for the better is a matter of opinion.'

'Is it, Hilda?'

'At any rate I had high hopes of you at that time. Extremely high hopes. So stick that in your memoirs, Rumpole.'

'Well, of course you did,' I didn't want to boast, 'when I got the Penge Bungalow job.'

'Yes, but what about me? What did I get exactly?' She looked at me, I thought, with a kind of amused pity. 'A husband who can't even keep his leg elevated.'

She left me then. I gently lowered my leg from the joint stool and put it on the ground in the regular writing position and did my best to describe the alarming weeks which led up to the trial of Simon Jerold on charges of double murder. As a tribute to the importance of the trial, and the great public interest in it, the Chief Justice, Lord Jessup, had consented to go slumming down the Old Bailey and try the case.

'It doesn't matter a scrap what you do or have to say,' Teddy Singleton of our chambers told me. 'Theobald Jessup will see your boy hangs as sure as next week will have a Thursday. There's a rumour he orders crumpets for tea at his club after he's passed a death sentence.'

I heard even more sinister rumours in Pommeroy's Wine Bar, suggesting that death sentences and sex produced the same results with the Lord Chief Justice. I also knew that Theo Jessup made jokes which I thought were in horribly bad taste. When a barrister wanted a short adjournment in a long murder trial to settle a will case, he said the prisoner should be removed from court as he probably didn't want to hear about 'due execution'. In an after-dinner speech, apparently intending to amuse the audience, he said that he had no trouble ending telephone calls because he was quite used to 'hanging up'. Whatever fate was in store for Simon, I couldn't bear the thought of him becoming a joke in an after-dinner speech.

As part of my preparation for the case I decided to take a preliminary look at Theobald Jessup. I dropped in to the Court of Criminal Appeal at which he was presiding. What I saw, in the central position, between the two 'bookends' of lesser judges, was a small, thick-set man with bright beady eyes, a nose that looked as though it might have been flattened in some long-distant football game or boxing bout, and skin the colour of old vellum. From time to time he dipped, as some judges still did in those days, into the scarlet depths of his gown and retrieved a small silver box on which he tapped. He then sniffed a pinch of snuff from the back of his hand. After he had absorbed whatever pleasure this practice brought him, he wiped his nose gently on an ornate silk handkerchief.

They were deciding an appeal against a conviction for murder, but it was the way the Lord Chief Justice began his judgement that I found, strangely enough, encouraging. 'It's a time-honoured precept of our criminal law,' he had a surprisingly high-pitched voice for a man so greatly feared, 'that it's far more intolerable and unjust for an innocent man to be convicted than for a guilty man, or indeed woman, to be let off.' After which hopeful start, there was a lengthy pause while the Lord Chief Justice took snuff. 'Even giving full weight to this cherished precept, I cannot find anything unsafe or unsound in the learned judge's summing up or the jury's verdict in this case.' After he had given his reasons, which appeared well argued, the two 'bookends' announced that they thoroughly agreed with 'every word that had fallen from the learned Chief Justice'. The subject of this decision, a small colourless man wearing spectacles, was removed from the dock and taken down the steps to meet his death.

*   *   *

99

'You never ask me out nowadays, Rumpole.' Daisy Sampson positively purred at me and then uttered a small sigh of regret. We were sitting side by side on a bench in the hallway of the Horseferry Road Magistrates' Court, waiting to do a matrimonial dispute which, because of a long list of drunk drivers and soliciting prostitutes, gave no immediate prospect of being called on for trial. 'And I've done all I can to give you my briefs in the most flagrant fashion.'

'Thank you.' The old joke was still around and I ignored it.

'The Timsons think the sun shines out of your backside, Rumpole. They're decent, hard-working minor criminals. And they should give you lots of jobs. So why don't you ask me out?'

'Because the last time I did that, you waltzed away from me. With Reggie Proudfoot!'

'Reggie Proudfoot? Don't talk to me about Reggie Proudfoot! He's not a gent, that Reggie Proudfoot, definitely not a gent.'

As this was the view I took of my fellow barrister, I looked more favourably on Daisy.

'You know what?'

'What?'

'He took me out to dinner. The Regent Palace Hotel. And at the end of quite a top-class meal with wine, he just fumbled. That's all he did!'

'Fumbled?'

'Pretended he'd forgotten his wallet. So I had to pay every penny. And do you think he ever paid me back?'

'I doubt it.'

'Your doubts, Rumpole, are fully justified. You'd never treat a girl like that, would you?'

100

'I'm sure I wouldn't.' I looked at her inviting red lips drawn back from the teeth that had never suffered restraint, the small heart-shaped face and the eyes full of mischief. I made a quick calculation of the fees I'd already received from small jobs plus what I was likely to gain from losing the Timson case, and thought of how much might be saved by more evenings boiling eggs on the gas ring. I decided to make a desperate bid for Daisy. 'Perhaps you'd like to have dinner with me?' I put down my stake.

'Perhaps I'd love it. The Regent Palace?'

'I was thinking more in terms of the Hibernian Hostelry.'

'Suits me.' Now she looked thoughtful. 'I've never seen where you live.'

'Off Southampton Row. I've got a bedsit.'

'What's it like?'

'Not too bad. It's got a gas ring and, well, of course, the bed's in the sitting room.'

'That sounds convenient.' She continued to smile.

'And my landlady,' I was doing my best to keep her entertained, 'owns a shop that sells trusses, wooden legs, sex manuals and rubber johnnies.'

'That sounds *very* convenient!' Daisy said, and by now she was laughing.

On which happy note, we settled on a date for dinner.

*   *   *

After an hour of a hearing, our matrimonial was adjourned for another month, during which the couple could live in silent loathing, communicating

101

with little notes left on the cooker or stuck to the parrot's cage, such as 'Get her down your office to cook your dinner. She seems to do everything else for you' or 'This bird is far better at conversation than you, you dumb person! I wish I'd married it!'

I was recovering from this weary day in court in Uncle Tom's room, going through, with considerable interest I have to say, the information that can be derived from the direction of bullet wounds. I was lifting a cup of instant coffee, run up for me in the clerk's room, when the door was flung open and Hilda Wystan came bounding in and sank down in a chair used by clients, when we had clients to visit us. She was, of course, the Hilda that was, and not the one introduced by me at the beginning of this chapter. That is to say, she took no exception to my having my feet firmly on the ground and didn't ask me to elevate either of my legs; instead she plumped herself down in our client's chair, blew out her cheeks so that her face assumed the proportions of a rather flushed balloon and said, 'Aren't you excited, Rumpole?'

Why should I be? Was she suggesting in the blowing out of her cheeks some sort of sensual intent. It was a question I was determined to duck.

'The Jerold murder business has just been fixed for three weeks' time. I called in at the clerk's room and Albert told me.'

'Well, he hasn't told me yet.'

'He likes to keep the good news to himself. I had quite a job squeezing it out of him.'

'I'm afraid it won't be particularly good news for Simon.'

'Of course not. Good news for me, though. I'll be there watching you.'

'And your father.'

'And watching Daddy, yes, of course. Although he's not always been frightfully keen on my interest in the law.'

'Has he not?' I remembered, with a pang of guilt, that it was Hilda's interest that had, it seemed, won me the junior brief in this famous murder trial.

'I did think of becoming a barrister, but Daddy said that Equity Court was not quite ready for a woman.'

'That's ridiculous!' Apart from his choice of me as his junior, I had so far found it difficult to defend the actions, or rather the inactive side, of Hilda's father. Now I felt a rush of sympathy for his daughter. 'Of course you should have been a barrister, if that's what you wanted.'

'Umm!' She looked thoughtful. 'Albert said there weren't the toilet facilities.'

'A trivial detail!' I assured her. 'Those things might have been arranged.'

'I thought about it, of course. But I decided it would be more sensible to get married.'

'There are plenty of married women barristers.'

'Oh, yes. But I thought marriage might be more satisfying than a life in the law. If I found someone who had a promising career, I could help them rise to the top.' There she gave a modest smile. 'The power behind the throne. You know the sort of thing?'

'I'm not quite sure I do know.'

'Well, if it were someone who might even become Head of Chambers, when Daddy goes of course . . .'

'So who,' for my own peace of mind I felt I

needed immediate clarification, 'are we talking about?'

'Don't worry your head about that now, Rumpole. You've got an important case starting. That's your foot on the first rung of the ladder, isn't it?'

*   *   *

Daisy was only half an hour late at the Hibernian Hostelry and she arrived in a neat black dress with dark eyeshadow and a determined smile. 'What a treat! I've been so looking forward to this.' We ordered the food of that period—prawn cocktail, steak and chips, topped off with Black Forest g,teau, washed down by a pink wine called Mateus Rosé, best remembered because people of that time saved the strange, circular bottles to make into side-table lamps. Daisy seemed happy enough and I, remembering how she had welcomed my landlady's convenient bedsit, was looking forward enormously to the after-dinner hour. I had prepared myself by visiting my landlady's shop and, instead of asking, in the old music-hall tradition, for something for the weekend, I bought three rubber johnnies, hoping for their immediate assistance.

But we were still spooning prawns out of glass bowls of pink sauce and Daisy was showing a remarkable interest in the Penge Bungalow trial. I told her that I'd been to see the judge in action.

'The hanging judge?'

'Oddly enough, there was something about him I found strangely encouraging. I thought we had views in common.'

'You're not telling me that you're going to start taking snuff, are you, Rumpole?'

'No, it's not the snuff. That's a disgusting habit. It's the presumption of innocence.'

Daisy Sampson, toying with her glass of Mateus Rosé, gave me an inquisitive look and said, 'You seem to be doing a lot of preparation for the Jerold case.'

'Do you think that's at all odd?'

'Just a bit. When your leader's told you that you won't be called on to say a single word. And he doesn't seem to take much notice of your suggestions.'

I told Daisy that I was trying to find an answer to Wystan's question to me.

'Oh, yes? And what question was that?' Daisy had both elbows on the table and, cradling her glass in both hands, smiled at me over it.

'If Simon didn't kill his father and "Tail-End" Charlie, who on earth did?'

'And do you think you've got any answers?'

'Not yet. We don't know enough about them. Everyone's convinced that Simon did it. They haven't asked nearly enough questions about the lives of Jerry and Charlie. Did they have any enemies?'

'Did they?'

'I don't know yet.'

'Is that why you were trying to get in touch with the other chap in the bomber—the navigator?'

'Did I tell you that?'

'Didn't you? You keep on talking about your great case.'

'I may have done. Anyway, he's no help. He died when the plane crashed and caught fire.' I was puzzled. I couldn't remember discussing David Galloway with Daisy. 'By some miracle, Jerry and Charlie escaped from the blazing plane.'

'So they were lucky?'

'Perhaps not so lucky. Death got them in the end.'

But we weren't there to discuss our cases. Halfway through the Black Forest g,teau I said, 'You wanted to see where I live.'

'Did I?' Daisy looked momentarily confused. 'Oh, yes, I believe I did.'

'And you said it would be so convenient having the bed in the sitting room.'

'Well, it would be, wouldn't it?'

'Exactly!' I agreed with enthusiasm. 'So would you like to see it now?'

'I suppose so.' She sounded doubtful. 'Is it far?'

'Not at all. Just off Southampton Row.'

'I mean, will it take long?'

'I suppose,' I smiled at her, 'just as long as we want it to take.'

'Oh, well then,' she said as I asked the waiter for the bill, which turned out to be unexpectedly steep on account of Daisy's insistence on a couple of gin and Its to precede the Mateus Rosé and a crème de menthe frappé to go after the pudding.

'I suppose I can manage it if it won't take too long.' It was not the most tender or most encouraging way to start a love affair, but I called a taxi to take us to the convenient bedsit of our choice.

I didn't know how my landlady would react to late-night visitors, so I asked Daisy to be quiet on the stairs. She reacted with exaggerated caution, tiptoeing up in solemn silence. When we got to the

106

top I threw open my door, gave a low bow and said, 'Welcome to my convenient home.'

I had honestly done my best with it. The electric fire had all bars glowing and it provided a warm welcome. The bed, with fresh sheets, was turned invitingly down. The papers on my desk were neatly arranged. I had done a good deal of dusting and even got a jug of slightly overblown chrysanths on the bedside table. I had considered scattering rose petals, but decided against it for reasons of economy.

'It's very nice, Rumpole.' Daisy gave it a quick look-around. 'I'm sure you're very happy here.'

'Very happy *now*,' I assured her, and planted a quick kiss on her scarlet lips.

She returned it briefly and then withdrew.

'I've got another Mateus Rosé,' I assured her. 'It's not exactly cold, but would you like a drink?' I looked at the glowing bars of the fire but, to my amazement, Daisy was consulting her watch.

'Terribly sorry, Rumpole. Can't possibly stay. This wretched party at the Four Hundred. Important clients. I promised to join them after dinner. Shop talk.' And she was off down the stairs with a clatter calculated to wake the dead.

It's right, of course, that these memoirs should contain disasters as well as triumphs. Now I had nothing to look forward to except an apparently hopeless trial at the Old Bailey. I sat on the bed and drank the wine, which was sweet, warm and did nothing to enhance the situation.

I don't know what you think about being young. To me, it's a time for growing used to disappointment.

107

12

The British can be relied on to produce regular events for the entertainment of the public, as much a part of our tradition as cricket at Lord's, stockings hung out on Christmas Eve and the pantomime on Boxing Day. A regular event, preferably in early autumn, is the famous murder trial. Staged in Court Number One at the Old Bailey, it plays to packed houses, news of it fills the daily papers and then, usually after 'guilty' headlines, it disappears into history, coming out perhaps in the *Notable British Trials* series, and then is remembered only by a few lawyers who are writing their memoirs, as I am, or by the families tragically involved.

R. v. *Jerold* could have been invented to fill this sensational slot. It is perhaps a sign of our times that in those faraway days there were only four courts at the Old Bailey. At the last count the number had gone up to eighteen. But even when trials were a great deal fewer Court Number One could always be relied on to produce an annual entertainment for the nation.

The summer was over, the children were back at school, the golden leaves of September drifted slowly down on a country anxious to read all about it in the Sunday tabloids, while the broadsheets were full of articles on 'Patricide since the story of Oedipus' and 'What the good people of Penge think about their sudden fame'. No wonder, with all those column inches to fill, the press benches were packed.

I sat behind my so-called leader, Hilda's daddy, who was carefully winding and unwinding the pink tape which came around his brief, an occupation which would concern him for much of the first day. I glanced up at the public gallery and saw Hilda, clearly excited and making herself comfortable in the front row of the dress circle.

Next to Wystan sat the prosecutor, the Chief Treasury Counsel, Thomas Winterbourne, protected by a wall of files and notebooks, underlining parts of his opening speech with variously coloured pencils. He was a large, untidy man who spoke in a deep, monotonous rumble which had, at times, a soporific effect like the distant sound of the sea. He was known to eat huge meals in the bar mess and mountains of sandwiches in Pommeroy's Wine Bar. He was also fond of gossip and fast motorbikes.

'Morning to you, Sherlock Rumpole. Think you know all the answers now, do you?' It was the bray of the wretched Reggie Proudfoot, one of the prosecution juniors, who was sitting beside me in the second row. 'I hear you've been doing more detective work. Wasting your time, my lad. Simply wasting your time.'

I had no intention of replying to Proudfoot's idiotic attack. Now an usher called, 'Silence! All stand!' and was met by the sound of a court filled with people of ranging degrees of mobility rising to their feet. In the ensuing clatter a small scarlet figure emerged from a door, bobbed us half a formal bow and half a small smile, and Lord Jessup composed himself on the bench and then gave a little nod as he took up a pencil and opened his notebook.

'The Queen against Jerold,' the clerk of the court intoned. 'Put up Simon Jerold.'

So Simon was 'put up' in the dock as though he was a glove puppet and part of a Punch and Judy show, and indeed, looking back on it, I suppose that was what he was, a hollowed-out figure manipulated to perform a plot worked out by lawyers. He looked pale and exhausted, lacking sleep and about to face a long and ancient procedure from which he suspected that no good would come.

I had met him with my leader earlier that day briefly in the cells, together with our solicitor, Barnsley Gough, and the industrious youth Bonny Bernard. Simon asked for a cigarette and Bernard gave him one, which he smoked awkwardly, punctuated by coughs, like someone who has just started the habit and means to continue with it for as long as he has left.

'Now, Jerold,' Hilda's daddy was doing his best to sound avuncular, 'you're not to worry.'

This instruction was so fatuous that it even produced a faint smile from the pallid young man we were defending.

'I mean, you're not to worry for today in any event. Mr Winterbourne will open the case for the prosecution, and he'll be perfectly fair, as he always is. There may just be time for a short witness this afternoon. You won't be surprised, I'm sure, if I don't ask any questions. Now, have you remembered at all about an attack by your father later that night? Anything that might have led you to defend yourself?'

'I told you. He never attacked me then. And I never shot him.' For a moment, Simon came to life.

'We'll see what you remember later on. In the meantime . . .'

'You're not going to ask any questions?' Simon spoke as though his worst fears had been confirmed.

'Let me tell you this, Jerold,' C. H. Wystan seemed about to take our client into his confidence, 'and this is something I have learned from a long life at the bar, a life, I may say, during which I have enjoyed a certain amount of success, that more cases are lost by lawyers asking questions than for any other reason. Is that not right, Mr Barnsley Gough?'

'Perfectly right, Mr Wystan.' Regrettably, our solicitor agreed.

'You see,' Wystan was about to explain, largely in words of one syllable, the situation as he saw it, 'the main facts of this case are agreed. You picked up a gun and threatened your father. The gun was taken away from you and in the morning your father was found dead in his chair, shot through his heart. If we start asking questions on these facts we will only irritate the judge and bore the jury.'

Then Simon emerged again from his shell of silence and said quite loudly, 'So you're not going to help me?'

Wystan stared at the prisoner, speechless, as though the young man had just snatched his wig and was ready to tear off his gown. Barnsley Gough did his best to mend matters by saying, 'You've got the best legal team to help you, Simon. Mr Wystan has a vast experience of these cases.'

I, to my eternal shame, said nothing, but vowed to give my client as much of my help as possible. C. H. Wystan looked at his watch and said, 'Quarter

112

past ten! We'd better be getting into court.' And so we all trooped out of the cells, up into the safer surroundings of Court Number One, where my learned leader would no longer have to speak to his client.

*   *   *

'Members of the jury,' Tom Winterbourne said in his opening speech, 'we shall call the ex-RAF officers who attended the theatrical night-out. All of those who survived will tell you that they saw Simon Jerold, the young man in the dock, pointing the Luger pistol at his father and, I'm afraid, threatening to kill.'

The appointed twelve (nine men and three women, in those distant days when only rate-payers could serve on juries) had entered the jury box looking as though they couldn't believe what had happened to them. They were minding their own business and leading their private lives when they were unexpectedly called upon to decide that year's sensational case. They had taken the oath to 'well and truly try the issues between our Sovereign Lady the Queen and the prisoner at the bar' and then sat looking serious but enigmatic as though they had little doubt, I suspected, in the contest between the Queen and Simon Jerold, who was most likely to win.

Hilda's daddy had charged me to take a note and I was determined to do at least that. So I was writing down almost every word of Winterbourne's, whose speech was being spoken slowly enough for my pen to follow.

'The prosecution case,' he rumbled and I wrote,

113

'is that when all the guests had gone, this boy, this unnatural son, came out of his bedroom, regained possession of this Luger pistol that I am holding up, Prosecution Exhibit One, and, seeing his father still sitting at the fireside, he stood over him and shot him through the heart as he sat there at his ease. So ended the life of one of our unsung wartime heroes.'

This was a passage I underlined heavily. At least we'd have something to argue about. I was going to call this to my leader's attention, but I found him in whispered conversation with our clerk, Albert, who had arrived with some news which caused the Wystan head to nod in sage agreement. Accordingly I kept what I thought might at least cause the rumbling Winterbourne some trouble until a more appropriate moment.

At the end of his opening speech, Winterbourne announced that he would first be calling one of the officers from the fatal evening, but there was a problem about the medical evidence. Dr Philimore, who carried out the post-mortems, was only available 'first thing tomorrow morning', after which he was flying out to Australia on an important case. The old rumbler hoped this wouldn't 'cause any inconvenience'.

'Mr Wystan?' The judge paused in the act of taking snuff to greet my leader in a friendly fashion.

'I'm in some difficulty myself, My Lord. My clerk has just told me I have an important application in the Court of Appeal tomorrow morning. A planning application.' He seemed unnaturally proud of the fact. 'However, there is no controversy about the medical evidence in this case, so my

114

learned junior, Mr Horace Rumpole, will be able to take a careful note of what the doctor says.'

'No controversy? I'm glad to hear it.' His vellum-coloured Lordship had now snuffled up the dark brown powder from the back of his hand and was dabbing his upper lip with the silk handkerchief. 'I'm delighted to hear that and I'm sure the jury are too.' Here he swivelled round to smile confidentially at the twelve honest citizens. 'Happily we are to be spared the confusion of medical men who may disagree, members of the jury.'

A day or two into the trial, they would have nodded wisely and smiled back at a judge anxious to woo them. Now they looked merely mystified.

The atmosphere in court changed when the first ex-RAF officer entered the witness box and the lawyers were no longer centre stage. He gave his name as Timothy Wardle and his occupation as salesman in the business of double-glazing. He had pink cheeks, curly hair and, since the war, he had put on weight so that his blue suit fitted tightly. He had the appearance of a middle-aged cherub who was finding the double-glazing business a hard nut to crack.

He had flown in Bristols during the war and knew Jerold and Weston. He lived in Sutton and he met both of them after the war at local events. It was at one of these that Jerold suggested the evening out in London. We heard the all-too-familiar story of the quarrel when Simon was summoned from his bed and the jury was told how he held the Luger pistol pointed at his father and uttered a threat to kill. Simon was disarmed by ex-Pilot Officer Benson and they didn't see him again.

115

The party broke up about an hour later and they went their separate ways.

'Thank you, Mr Wardle.' The prosecutor seemed sincerely grateful, and the judge asked my leader if he had any questions.

'The magazine!' I whispered at the back of Wystan's left shoulder. 'Ask him about the magazine!'

'What was that, Rumpole?' he muttered without turning round.

'It's in the notes I gave you. Ask him about the magazine.'

It seemed I might just as well have been enquiring about the latest copy of the *Tatler*, and at that moment the judge told us he had been looking at the clock and, it being just on four, he intended to pack up for the day. 'The jury have no doubt had a great deal to digest. However, as there appears to be a disagreement in the defence team, perhaps the prosecution would have Mr Wardle available tomorrow morning when you, Mr Wystan, return from the Court of Appeal. Is that agreeable to you, Mr Winterbourne?'

'Certainly, My Lord,' the agreeable rumble came from the other side of the court.

'Very well then, ten-thirty tomorrow morning, members of the jury.' At which, we were all upstanding and the Lord Chief Justice deprived us of his company.

'I just thought that the evidence about the magazine was important,' I tried to explain to Hilda's daddy as we left the court.

'We agree with everything that happened at that party, as I've tried to tell you, Rumpole.' My leader was a little tetchy. 'Now you promise me you won't

116

attack the doctor's evidence.'

'Of course I won't attack his evidence.'

'Excellent! I'll be back from the Appeal Court as soon as I can be. It is, as I'm sure you realize, an important matter. Do you think the client understands that?'

The client, when we said goodbye to him that day, seemed to understand nothing, or care very much either. He stared at the ground between his feet in silence. But I felt a kind of excitement, as though the next day offered a chance, if I could only grab it, of great importance in the Rumpole career.

13

In many cases to come I was to argue, across a crowded courtroom, on the topics of bloodstains, the direction of wounds and the time of death with Dr Ackerman, whom I christened 'King of the Morgues' and whose company I greatly enjoyed. His predecessor and teacher was the great Dr Philimore, soon to become Sir Percival, whose pronouncements on matters of forensic medicine were to be received with the respect paid to Holy Writ. At the time of the Penge Bungalow trial the future Sir Percival had already assumed the mantle of major prophet. He was of no great height, broad-shouldered and deep-chested, he wore the sort of greyish beard favoured by the late King George V and he spoke with such certainty and persuasion that few judges, let alone barristers, felt able to contradict or even interrupt him.

He went through his evidence in chief. Jerold died from a bullet wound in the heart. Death would have occurred very shortly after the shot. He was unable to give the court an accurate time of death, but it must have occurred at least six hours before the body was brought into the mortuary, where notes were taken of its temperature and the state of rigor. The wound had clearly been made by the German bullets preserved and exhibited. Much the same diagnosis appeared in his post-mortem examination of 'Tail-End' Charlie.

During his evidence, I was looking, from time to time, at the door of the court, afraid that my leader might return and impose his silence on the proceedings. I was also terrified I would forget what I had to ask on that most public of stages, lose my thread and make a complete fool of myself. I was lost in a dream of disaster when I heard Winterbourne rumble a grateful, 'Thank you, Dr Philimore,' and I saw the great man turn to leave the witness box.

Then I stood up, and miraculously the mists cleared, and I was able to say, 'Just a moment, Doctor. I have a few questions for you,' almost as calmly as if I were ordering a glass of Château Thames Embankment in Pommeroy's.

'Mr um, er . . .' The judge was searching through his papers in the hope that somewhere he might have made a note of my name. He found it and looked at it as though he couldn't believe his eyes. 'Er, Mr Rumpole. We understood from your learned leader that you agreed with the medical evidence.'

'Of course, My Lord. We have just a few questions.'

'Are you asking me to wait for Mr Wystan to return?'

'Oh, certainly not, My Lord. I cannot possibly ask you to delay the trial. That wouldn't be in the public interest, and we have agreed not to attack the doctor's evidence.' This, at least, was true. 'I'm merely putting a few points for clarification. And so we may have the benefit of Dr Philimore's enormous knowledge and experience.' I was, as a youth, capable of being quite intolerable.

The judge screwed up his eyes and gave me his quizzical look, probably asking himself, 'Who is this whippersnapper, this young white wig who talks to me as though he's been knocking round the Old

120

Bailey for the last thirty years?' Then, after a preparatory pinch of snuff, he muttered a reluctant, 'Oh, very well then,' before making use of the silk handkerchief.

'Doctor, death after being shot through the heart isn't necessarily instant, is it?' Here a page from Philimore's own book on the subject flashed before my eyes. 'I'm sure you've written about victims who may have walked at least several yards.'

'That is so, yes.' The great man looked a little wary, as though I was about to lead him into a trap.

'So we're agreed. Now, might the witness be given the photograph of the room with the dead man in the armchair?' The relevant photograph was handed up to him and again the doctor glanced at it as though it was an impertinent and unnecessary addition to his evidence. I waited for the jury to find the photograph in their folders and then continued, with a calm I felt almost alarming, 'You see the dead man is on the left of the fireplace?'

'Yes, I see that, thank you,' the Doctor added, exaggerating the tolerance due to a white wig.

'Behind him is an open door that leads to a short hallway and the front door of the bungalow.'

'I see that too.'

'You will also see that the bloodstains have been circled.'

'Yes, they have.'

'And is there not a bloodstain, which we are all agreed is of the same group as the deceased's blood, on the wall of the hallway?'

'I see that, yes.'

'So, is it not possible that the deceased may have

121

been shot, got up from his chair and moved at least that distance into the hallway?'

'Yes, that is possible.' The doctor seemed a little surprised that he had to admit it.

'Or might not this be possible, that he was in the hall, opening the door to someone who shot him, he bled in the hallway and he returned to his chair to die?'

It was the first of the two points I had to make. The fear returned. If I got the wrong answer, I had done nothing but further damage an already hopeless case, bored the jury, irritated the judge and might well be thrown out of chambers for insubordination. The clock ticked, the judge sat motionless with his pencil raised, the jury were looking at the photograph and time stood still. And then, at long last, it came—Dr Philimore's answer, now given a little reluctantly.

'I couldn't rule out that possibility either.'

I came back to my senses. The fear gurgled away like dirty bathwater. I had more questions for the great oracle, but I felt surprisingly calm about the result. 'Dr Philimore, you've made a study of the path of bullets in a body?'

'Yes, that is so.' He spoke as though everybody knew about his book *The Causes of Death.*

'If the gun were held higher than the wound and so shot downwards, there would be a downward trajectory?'

'There would, obviously.'

'But if the assailant and the victim were both standing at about the same height, the trajectory would be straight, as it is in this case?'

'That is what I found, yes.' He said it with a small sigh, as though the fact should be

122

self-evident.

'So can we rule out the theory that the assailant here was standing and shooting downwards at a man seated in the chair?'

'I think we can, yes.'

'Let me just remind the court, and you of course, Dr Philimore, of my friend Mr Winterbourne's opening speech.' I picked up my underlined notebook and took longer than necessary to find the quotation, hoping to increase the expectation of a bombshell. 'Ah, here it is,' I said some time after I'd found it, and then I quoted the rumbler: " 'Seeing his father still sitting at the fireside, he stood over him and shot him through the heart as he sat . . .' " Then I asked for Prosecution Exhibit One. So, for the first, but certainly not the last, time, I had a weapon in my hand in the Old Bailey. I stood holding it and pointed it downwards in the direction of Reggie Proudfoot, seated beside me. This provoked one of the many rebukes I have since received from judges.

'I think you have made your point, Mr um . . . Rumpole. We can do without the pantomime.'

'With the greatest respect to Your Lordship, this is no pantomime. This is a vital part of the prosecution case. It couldn't have happened like that, could it, Dr Philimore? In view of the trajectory of the bullet?' I stood amazed at my courage in arguing with the Lord Chief Justice.

There was a pause and then the great expert said, 'No. I don't think it could.'

'Now, if we could turn to the case of Charlie Weston.'

'In view of the fact that the man is no longer alive,' the judge sounded displeased, 'I think it

123

would be more appropriate, Mr Rumpole, if you called him Charles.'

'I'm much obliged to Your Lordship.' I was in a high mood after Dr Philimore's last answer and ready to be obliging. 'To *Charles* Weston.' I flipped through the volume of photographs and there was 'Tail-End' Charlie, a small wiry man, the cheeky grin I imagined he once wore relaxed in death. 'Would I be right in saying that you found the same sort of trajectory of the bullet as in the case of Jerry Jerold?'

'That is right.'

'So he was probably shot by someone standing up as he was standing.'

'I would say so.'

'Now we know from Mr Winterbourne's opening that Charles Weston wasn't found until the cleaning lady, who had a key, arrived at nine-thirty the next morning.'

'I believe that is so.'

'And so we can assume he was alone in his bungalow when he died.'

'If you say so.' The great man sighed as though this was taking far too long and he was anxious to get off to Australia.

'Not if I say so, Doctor. If anyone else was with him, it will be for the prosecution to prove it. It seems likely that someone rang the front door bell, Charles Weston went to the hall to open it to whoever it was who shot him and he fell dead in the hallway.'

'That seems the most likely explanation.'

'I'm much obliged.' I was in fact truly grateful. 'So if we accept that, we can't rule out that both of these men died in exactly the same way, opening

124

their front doors to an unknown caller.'

'As I have said, we can't rule out that possibility.'

'Thank you, Dr Philimore.' I sat down with all the satisfaction of a trainee lion tamer who has emerged from the cage of the most ferocious of the big cats with not one single scratch. Of course, Winterbourne did his best to retrieve the situation with such questions as 'Whatever positions the two men had taken up, you agree that the father was shot by that pistol?' And having got the answer, 'Yes,' he reminded the jury that Simon had picked up the gun earlier in the evening with a threat to kill. After he'd sat down, with my new-found confidence undiminished I made an application. 'My Lord, Your Lordship asked that the witness Mr Wardle might be here this morning in case we had any questions.'

'In case your learned leader had any questions, Mr Rumpole.' The judge now seemed, rather to his regret, able to remember my name.

'And in my leader's absence I am asking to put a question to Mr Wardle.'

Here the judge sighed; again it was only the first of many sighs of discontented resignation I was to hear from judges over the years at the Old Bailey. 'I don't suppose you can object to that, Mr Winterbourne.' Unhappily for the judge, the prosecutor couldn't and the chubby and cherubic ex-pilot officer, now double-glazing salesman, re-entered the witness box.

'Mr Wardle, you told us yesterday that you saw Simon Jerold pick up the Luger pistol and talk about killing . . .'

' "You're so keen on teaching people to kill people. I promise you I'll kill the first of you that

125

touches me. So you'd better watch out." ' The judge supplied the threatening words from his notebook, for which I thanked him profusely.

'I'm much obliged for your help, My Lord. Now, Mr Wardle, Simon Jerold will say that the magazine with bullets in it was kept separate from the gun. It was somewhere else on that mantelpiece.'

'I'm not sure about that.'

'You're not sure?'

'No.'

'But it may have been so?'

'It may well have been.'

Now there was a small disturbance. The door swung open and Hilda's daddy returned to court. Seeing me on my feet and asking questions, he gave me a look of something like horror. This didn't deter me. 'Did you see Simon load the magazine into the pistol after he had picked it up?'

'No.' The witness was clear. 'I didn't see him doing anything like that.'

'You're sure you didn't?'

'Quite sure.'

'So, for all you know, Simon may have been holding an unloaded gun when he made those threats?'

'He may have been.'

This was a cause for more gratitude. 'Thank you very much, Mr Wardle,' I said. And then I turned before I sat down to look at my client in the dock and I saw, for the first time in the pale face of this young man facing death, the flicker of a smile.

*　　　　*　　　　*

126

There was no smile, however, on the face of my learned leader when we broke off for the lunchtime adjournment. He was, on the whole, a gentle person and he looked at me more in sorrow than in anger. 'I gave you strict instructions, Rumpole,' he said, 'not to ask any questions.'

'Quite right.' I couldn't keep a note of triumph out of my voice. 'But I thought of one or two points that might help us. I'll give you a full note.'

'I shall read it, of course, but I give you fair warning, Rumpole, I don't intend to leave you alone again. This is a case which calls for *tact*, Rumpole, and the guidance of a leading counsel the judge will trust.'

'Trust to lose politely?' was what I felt like saying, but I was silenced by the clear, bell-like tones of my leader's daughter, who had descended from the public gallery to greet us. To her father's surprise and disappointment, she gave me a hearty hug. 'Well done, Rumpole!' And after suggesting we all had lunch at the little Italian place opposite, she added, 'Rumpole scored a couple of direct hits in his cross-examination, Daddy.' At which my leader looked more sorrowful than ever. He might have said more, and we might have had that lunch in the little Italian place opposite the Old Bailey, but our solicitor, Barnsley Gough, with young Bonny Bernard in attendance, joined us with some news. Our client had sent him a message: he wanted a conference urgently in the cells beneath our feet. Lunch with Hilda was postponed indefinitely.

127

14

'I have thought about it. And I've made up my mind. No matter what you tell me!'

We had gone down from the courtroom level and passed the old door of Newgate Prison, with names carved on it by long-gone customers on their way to the gallows. We had seen the screws consuming doorstep-sized sandwiches and gone into the small interview room to which they brought our client. As he sat down, he asked Bonny Bernard for 'one of those Capstan full-strengths'. He was no longer listless and silenced by terror. It was then he said something extraordinary. 'I want Mr Rumpole to do my case.'

'Have you really thought about it? It won't look good in the eyes of the Lord Chief, not good at all.' It was Barnsley Gough who said it, and then our client replied in the words I've quoted at the start of this chapter.

'But Mr Rumpole *is* doing your case, Jerold.' Hilda's daddy started off in the appeasing voice of a lawyer trying to reach an agreement, a way out which would satisfy everyone. 'He is helping me, as I said, by taking a careful note, and of course *we* shall discuss your case together. Mr Rumpole is an important part of your defence team.'

'But I don't want *you* on my defence team, Mr C. H. Wystan. I only want Mr Rumpole.'

'Mr Barnsley Gough, had you any idea about this?' Wystan seemed to be crying for help.

'The client did mention it. I told him it was out of the question.'

'Quite out of the question, for whatever reason . . .' This was Wystan speaking.

'I'll tell you the reason.' Simon broke into the lawyers' conversation with a new confidence. 'Because you are not going to do a thing for me. You said you wouldn't ask any questions and, what's more, you didn't, did you, Mr Wystan? You just sat there like a pudding.'

'A pudding?' My leader couldn't believe his ears and he called on our solicitor for confirmation. 'Did he say "*pudding*"?'

'I believe he did,' Barnsley Gough had to admit. 'The young man's not quite himself, of course.'

'I am quite myself,' Simon told us all. 'In fact, I feel much more like myself again. Mr Rumpole wanted you to ask about the magazine, didn't he? I could hear him from the dock. He's got a loud whisper, has Mr Rumpole. "Ask about the magazine," he was saying. "It's in my notes." And what did you do, Mr C. H. Wystan? Sat there like a pudding and did nothing for me. Mr Rumpole asked the questions and got a good answer. I never loaded the gun.'

' "Like a pudding" again.' Wystan turned once more to Barnsley Gough as though he couldn't believe his ears.

'And then who got the doctor to admit I couldn't have shot Dad in the way they said? Mr Rumpole! When you were away on other business.'

This outburst seemed to have exhausted Simon. He had felt the surge of anger which no doubt overcame him when the ex-RAF officers attacked him for having missed the war. He sat in silence, smoking his Capstan full-strength, which he now held delicately between his fingers. From then on

130

my leader ignored him, only addressing himself to Mr Barnsley Gough. 'It's clear, isn't it, Mr Gough? Our client has lost faith in his appointed counsel.'

'I'm afraid that would seem to be the case, Mr Wystan.'

'And he used unpleasant, insulting language.' The pudding had clearly stuck in my leader's gullet.

'He is under some strain, of course,' Barnsley Gough was fair enough to say again.

'Of course he is. We all understand that. But he must realize I can't continue to represent him if he has no confidence in me.'

'Oh, I'm sure he doesn't want that . . .' Barnsley Gough tried to say, but he was interrupted by Simon.

'Yes, I do want that. I want it very much indeed.'

'Then, with that further clear indication of the client's wishes, I shall withdraw from the case. Rumpole, you will no doubt withdraw with me.'

But Simon repeated, 'I want Mr Rumpole to stay.'

I looked at my leader and I have to admit I felt sorry for him. He had given me my first important job and done nothing worse than adopt a course of masterly inactivity which he thought of as the most tactful way of living through a hopeless case. And yet there were more important things in life than feeling sorry for Hilda's daddy. Simon helped me by repeating his instructions: 'I want Mr Rumpole to stay and do my case!'

'Rumpole,' Wystan spoke to me as though he had never heard a word from Simon, 'when a leading counsel withdraws from a case, his junior naturally withdraws also.'

'Is there a law about that?' I was doubtful

enough to ask.

'No law. It's just one of the finest traditions of the great profession of the bar.'

Wystan was reluctant to speak of such matters in the presence of a solicitor, so I spoke rapidly, and in a low voice, 'The finest traditions of our great profession,' I told him, I hoped quietly, 'may not be so important as saving Simon's life.'

'If you think that,' Wystan looked as though I had said something deeply shocking, 'then all I can say is you'd better ask to see the judge.'

*   *   *

With his wig off and finishing a fat cigar, the Lord Chief Justice seemed smaller, almost insignificant. He sat in his room, which was decorated with photographs of the prize pigs he reared on his farm on the Berkshire Downs, and listened with half a smile to Wystan's long complaint in which the word 'pudding' was to be heard and often repeated. He cut short the tale of woe, when it was, I suppose, about three-quarters of the way through. 'I understand completely, Wystan,' he said. 'I believe your position has become untenable and you're entitled to withdraw and Mr . . .' there followed the inevitable 'umm . . . Rumpole.'

'I'm going to stay,' I told His Lordship. 'I mean, our client wants me to do the case.'

'Then your client's wishes must be respected. How long since you've been called to the bar?'

'Eighteen months,' was what I had to tell him.

'Eighteen months! It was fifteen years before I did my first defence in a murder case. The Hastings strangler, if you remember it, Wystan? Of course I made a complete balls-up of it. Merely tightened the noose round the client's neck. I'd better have young Jerold up in court and warn him of the dangers. Thank you for keeping me in the picture, Wystan. No doubt you'll find a more profitable occupation than a murder on Legal Aid. By the way, Winterbourne,' here the judge addressed the prosecutor, who was entitled to be present at the meeting and had nothing much to lose, 'how long is this trial going to last?'

'It'll be more weeks, My Lord. We've got all the witnesses from the party and the police evidence. And if the defence call the boy . . .'

'Two more weeks?' The Lord Chief Justice seemed surprised. 'Cases were much shorter in my day. Well, I suppose we'll get through it!'

As he left, I was hoping against hope that Simon would live through it as well as the rest of us.

*   *   *

Simon was brought up from the cells and, in the absence of the jury, the situation was explained to him with painstaking clarity by the Lord Chief Justice. Simon's leader, a man of huge experience and the highest of reputations, had withdrawn from the case. He, the judge, was surprised beyond belief that Simon Jerold should have caused Mr C. H. Wystan's departure. That left young Mr Umm . . . (He seemed longer than ever searching for my name, as though to emphasize my obscurity and complete absence of reputation around the courts of law.) Ah! (The Lord Chief Justice had found my name, but pronounced it with some difficulty) Mr Rum—yes, Rumpole. A barrister only recently called, who was unknown, as far as he could gather, around the Old Bailey. Usually a junior withdrew from the case with his leader, but this young man had chosen to offer himself as counsel for the defence. It had to be said that he had asked a few questions with reasonable confidence, but he had clearly never before dealt with a case of such importance. Now, would Simon Jerold like an adjournment in order that a barrister of similar standing to Mr Wystan be found who might be prepared to act?

'No, sir.' Simon spoke clearly and with determination from the dock. 'I'd like to get on with it. And I want Mr Rumpole to do my case.'

It was an odd moment when Simon, and not the judge, seemed to dominate the proceedings. The judge, without even having taken snuff, blew his nose on the silk handkerchief and then wiped it carefully. After a short period of contemplation, staring at the apparently determined young man in the dock, he gave in. 'Well, I suppose you're entitled to the counsel of your choice. Have you any objections to Mr Rumpole conducting the case for the defence, Mr Winterbourne?'

The prosecutor rumbled to his feet and, with a knowing smile, said, 'None whatever, My Lord.'

'I thought you might say that.' The judge smiled back, but his smile died when he said, 'Mr Rumpole, you now take over the sole responsibility for this young man's defence.'

As I stood to thank His Lordship, I heard Reggie Proudfoot, in a stage whisper beside me, say how delighted he'd be to see me make a complete pig's breakfast of the job. Then I sat down while the jury were called back into court and

134

my sole responsibility began.

So, that is how I came to do the Penge Bungalow Murders alone and without a leader.

15

'Why did you have to put that disgusting bit about the Sampson woman in your memoirs, Rumpole?'

Hilda's question alerted me to the danger of a man leaving his memoirs free and open about the matrimonial home. Perhaps I should always write in chambers in future. For the moment, however, I answered her as well as I could. 'Because it wasn't disgusting. Unhappily, nothing in the least disgusting occurred. I'm trying to tell the truth, Hilda, to be honest about my failures.'

'Well, you'd better not be a failure next month.'

Her remark puzzled me. 'I'm not expecting any particularly important trial.'

'You'll have to be on your best behaviour, Rumpole. Dodo Mackintosh will be here and some of the girls we were at school with. Sandy Butterworth and Emma Glastonbury and the Gage twins and lots more. We've got tickets for *Phantom of the Opera* and then we're coming back here for a slap-up supper.'

'You mean Dodo Mackintosh will be staying?' I was somewhat daunted by the prospect.

'She likes you, Rumpole. She does her best to help. Don't you remember, she makes cheesy bits for your chambers' parties?'

'Which was the one who said it was such a pity I never got made a circus judge?'

'Circuit judge, Rumpole. Heather Gage said she was sorry your face didn't fit with the powers that be.'

'Thank God for that. I don't have a face for

the circus.'

'The Gage twins' father was a circuit judge, so of course he knows all about it.'

'And I bet he never, at my tender age, stood up to do a double murder without a leader at the Old Bailey.'

'He lives in Wimbledon.'

'That's exactly what I mean. So all your school friends will be coming back here after an evening at the theatre?'

'The whole jolly crowd of them.'

'I can only hope,' I was remembering another after-theatre party, 'that no one gets shot.'

*　　　*　　　*

'Now we can really talk.' My first day alone in court hadn't presented too many problems. Simon's statement to the police was put in and read. We had the evidence of finding the pistol in the dustbin. The Lord Chief wanted to rise early: it was a Friday and he said, with apparent generosity, we could have the afternoon off 'so Mr Rumpole could prepare himself to take over the defence'. In reality, I suspected, he was longing to visit his prize pigs. The ex-officers who had made up the theatre party were to be called next week. This was just as well, because I had to put our defence to them and I hadn't as yet any idea of what our defence could be. I knew that if I went back to my chambers, I should find C. H. Wystan skulking in his tent, no doubt determined to banish me from Equity Court for ever, so I took the opportunity of another meeting in the interview room down below and hoped for help from Simon. Barnsley Gough had remembered an important meeting of his local Masons' lodge, so Bonny Bernard was left with me in sole charge of the case.

'You were a schoolboy when the war broke out. Old enough to remember . . .'

'Oh, yes. Quite old enough.'

'Your father joined up early?'

'Very early. He was excited about it. Enthusiastic. I remember he was so pleased with himself when he was made a pilot officer. He said he got through his training first class. He was so proud, the first time he came home on leave in the full uniform.'

Simon had changed. His words, held back in the gloomy conferences with Hilda's daddy, seemed unblocked and came tumbling out of him. He had, I suppose, achieved a legal triumph and changed barristers in midstream. The terrifying fact was that I felt sure that he thought, with me in charge, he was set fair for an acquittal. Little did he know that, on that Friday afternoon, the Rumpole head was quite empty of ideas. Had I made an enemy of C. H. Wystan and invited my exit from Equity Court just in order to achieve the ghastly result Hilda's daddy could have arrived at with no trouble at all? I did my best to dismiss such unhelpful thoughts from my mind and concentrated on listening to Simon.

'And were you proud of him?'

'Of course I was! A schoolboy with a pilot officer, a man with wings on his uniform, for a father. Of course. I used to boast at school about him.'

'In the early years of the war, during the Blitz, you were living in a London suburb?'

139

'I know. It was exciting, wasn't it? Skies lit up with fires. Streets full of broken glass. And Mum and I used to go down the shelter with our gas masks and listen to Gracie Fields singing on the portable.'

'"Walter! Walter! Lead me to the altar. It's either the workhouse or you."' In the memory of those old days, I burst into song, perhaps unexpectedly, as the door opened and one of the screws, still chewing a sandwich, said, 'You all right, Mr Rumpole?'

'Perfectly all right, thank you. I'm afraid I sang rather too loudly.'

'Don't worry, sir. We don't get much singing of any sort. Not down here.' And so the friendly screw left us.

'And your mother?' I gave Simon my full attention.

'Oh, she was proud too. I'm sure she loved Dad. Particularly in uniform.'

I remembered my uniform as a member of the ground staff. It hadn't won me many conquests, apart from the brief but memorable love affair with WAAF Bobby O'Keefe. But back to business. 'The chaps at the party after the Palladium, were they friends of your father's in the early days?'

'Charlie of course. And Peter Benson.'

'Benson was the one who relieved you of the pistol?'

'He did that, yes. You were right, though, I never loaded it.'

'I know. How often did you see this man Benson?'

'He lived somewhere in Sutton. He and Dad used to go out to the pub when they were on leave.

Then they'd come back to the bungalow and Mum would do them scrambled eggs. Charlie was with them sometimes.'

'So it was quite a happy war?' How could all this love and pride, evenings at the pub and scrambled eggs, end in a boy who murdered his father facing another kind of death?

'At first it seemed happy. We were proud of Dad and he seemed proud of himself. Then he got worse.'

'What do you mean, worse?'

'Silent. Not speaking or flying out at me and Mum. He made her cry, often. Mum said he couldn't sleep. He got miserably drunk when he went to the pub instead of just cheerful.'

'When he went to the pub with Benson?'

'Yes, with him, and Charlie sometimes.'

'And this was?'

'When he was doing those raids over France. Almost every night, he told us, in the Bristol . . . It was as though he had a premonition or something.'

'A premonition?'

'Before they told us his plane had crashed over France, Mum often said it was as though he could see it coming. And he had changed his mind about the war.'

'You mean, he didn't think he should be fighting it?'

'Not that. I'm sure he was a loyal officer, obeyed orders and all that sort of thing. He got miserable because it was a war we couldn't win.'

'He told you that?'

'And Mum. He said the Germans had all the power, ". . . look at the way they got the whole of Europe". So many of his friends had been killed on raids and he thought there was no longer any sense in it. Oh, he said Hitler didn't really want to conquer the British Empire. We should make peace and let him get on with "kicking those bloody Russian Communists up the arse".'

'But he went on flying raids over occupied France?'

'I told you, he was a loyal officer. He wouldn't have done anything else.'

'All the same, you weren't meant to talk like that in the war, were you?'

'That's what worried Mum. She told me not to tell anyone at school. Of course, she never told her friends.'

There was a silence as I tried to digest this information and then I changed the subject. 'Talking of friends, does the name David Galloway mean anything to you?'

'He was Dad's navigator.'

'And apparently the only one to die when the plane was shot down.'

'I think he came to the bungalow a few times. He was a quiet sort of bloke. He didn't have much to say for himself. I think he was more Peter Benson's friend than Dad's. He was nice to me, though, brought me off-ration Mars Bars.'

'A generous sort?'

'With Mars Bars.'

'And then you heard your father's plane had been brought down?'

'Dad was missing, believed dead. It was then Mum began to tell me about the premonitions.'

'He felt he was going to die?'

'He got scared of going on raids. That's what she told me. Really scared. So scared that he couldn't sleep at night. In a way the news came as a sort of relief to her. It was all over. He wasn't going to suffer any more of that terrible fear.'

'Then your mother . . .'

'Shopping round Oxford Street, a stupid buzz bomb. A chance in a thousand. She'd done no harm to anyone. Do you wonder why I hate war, Mr Rumpole?'

'No, I don't wonder.'

'My Aunt Harriet came over from Chertsey to look after me. Then the news came. Dad and Charlie had been picked up by the allies in France. The war was over and he and Charlie came home.'

'Were you glad to see him?'

'Of course I was glad. You don't know my Aunt Harriet, Mr Rumpole.'

I looked at him, amazed. This boy, up till now paralysed, as his father had been, by the fear of death, had made what was almost a joke. 'And how did he seem to you when he got back?'

'He'd changed again.'

'For the worse?'

'He was just like he'd been at the start of the war, full of pride and enthusiasm. We didn't hear anything about making peace with Hitler.'

'Did he tell you much about what had happened to him?'

'He said the plane was damaged by anti-aircraft fire and he made a crash-landing. He and Charlie got out before it burst into flames.'

'And the navigator didn't?'

'That's right.'

'And then what did he say happened?'

'Well, it was always a bit vague. He said they tried to hide but they were eventually captured by

143

the Germans. They were sent to a prison in Germany until . . . well, until the war was almost over. Then they managed to get out and they were picked up by the American 7th Army. Anyway, they were brought home.'

'So he was a prisoner of war?'

'I think they both were.'

'You and your mother never got any notification of that. You never heard from the Red Cross, for instance?'

'No.' Simon shook his head. 'I suppose it all got a bit chaotic. In the last years of the war.'

'What did he tell you about his time as a prisoner?'

'Nothing really. I don't think he wanted to remember. Oh, he told us about the pistol he'd found on the body of a dead German officer. After they'd got out of whatever prison that was.'

The cursed weapon, I thought, the cause of so many deaths, brought back as a trophy of war. 'The rest of the collection on the mantelpiece, did he bring that back as well?'

'Oh, no. He decorated the mantelpiece as soon as he was a pilot, at the start of the war. When he was gone, we kept it there out of respect for him, I suppose. Then he put up the German pistol.'

'One thing puzzles me.'

'What's that?'

'Your father went through a time, you said, when he hated war and was afraid of flying. But then he quarrelled with you at the party, saying you shouldn't have missed that war and you ought to enjoy training for the next one.'

'That was what he was like when he came home. The war had just been a glorious victory and he'd

144

lived dangerously. After that I think he found the job at the bank pretty dull. All his excitement was in the past.'

'You got on well together?'

'Not all the time. He was always saying the war would have made a man of me.'

'What did you tell him?'

'That I didn't want to crash planes or shoot German officers and I just hoped it didn't happen again. I wanted him to stop talking about it.'

'And that made him angry?'

'Very angry at times.'

I sat a while in thought. Then I found Simon looking at me, his moment of confidence gone, his eyes desperate for reassurance. 'Have I given you what you wanted? Told you the right things, have I?'

'I'm sure what you've told me will be very useful, yes.' This was a lie. I wasn't sure of any such thing. I just wanted him to have some small hope to cling on to during his trial.

16

'Mr Wystan wanted to see you as soon as you got back from court.' Our clerk, Albert Handyside, uttered the words I'd been dreading, and he didn't make them any less unnerving by adding, 'It's been nice knowing you, Mr Rumpole. I hope our paths may cross again some time in the future.'

So I knocked politely and entered our leader's room with the grimmest forebodings and was surprised by the apparent warmth of my welcome.

'So there you are, Rumpole! Sit down. Can I offer you a glass of sherry wine?' C. H. Wystan produced a decanter, otherwise kept under lock and key in his cupboard, a glass of which was offered to special clients on special occasions. One far-off night at Keble College I had consumed, with a couple of dissolute theology students (one of whom has since become Bishop of Bath and Wells), a couple of bottles each of the college sherry, causing the room to sway and pitch like the *Titanic* on a bad night and much staggering to the lavatory. Since then I have had a particular horror of sherry, which seems to me as sickly as port, sticking faithfully to Pommeroy's Very Ordinary and the pints of Guinness favoured by Albert Handyside. This was a situation, however, where I had to thank our leader profusely, swallow some of the sweet and sickly fluid and hope the room would at least keep still. C. H. Wystan took a sip, smacked his lips and said, 'Wonderful stuff, this Amontillado!'

'Oh, yes,' I assured him, 'wonderful stuff.'

'Hard to get a decent glass of sherry these days.'

147

'Indeed,' I was prepared to agree, 'very hard.'

'Stocks of this particular label are running low. I have to save it for special occasions.'

Was this a special occasion, the dismissal of a rebellious member of Equity Court? I did my best to look gratified.

'One can understand,' C. H. Wystan was sitting back in his chair, thoughtfully running his finger round the rim of his glass, 'I think I can understand the feelings of our client in *R.* v. *Jerold*.'

I didn't particularly like the reference to 'our client', but I was in no position to argue. 'I think I can understand him too,' I said.

'After all it can't be pleasant to have to face the possibility of a death sentence.'

'I don't think,' how could I disagree with him?, 'that would be pleasant at all.'

'So naturally his judgement was clouded. He couldn't understand the tactics we had decided to adopt.'

'*We* had decided?' I couldn't help it, I had struck a disagreeable note. To compensate for this I took a large gulp of sherry.

'Of course, I mean that, as your leader, *I* had decided. Tactics are always a matter for the leader. You are there to assist me with a full note.'

'Just remind me,' I couldn't help asking, 'what were our tactics exactly?'

'Not to irritate the court and antagonize the jury by taking bad points or challenging evidence we agreed with. Then we hoped he would remember the incident more clearly.'

'Yes, of course.' I'm afraid I said it as though I needed reminding. 'You decided not to challenge any of the witnesses.'

148

'One can understand the client's anxiety.' C. H. Wystan was clearly in a forgiving mood.

'He seemed to be less anxious when I asked questions.' I couldn't help saying this, and as I said it I knew it was a mistake and a respectful silence would not have antagonized the court, in the person of our Head of Chambers, who was about to decide my fate. 'When you were away and I got the evidence about the entry of the bullets, and the separate magazine, he seemed quite grateful.'

'Can you be absolutely sure,' now C. H. Wystan was smiling in what I took to be a lofty and somewhat patronizing manner, 'that either of those questions will make any significant difference to the result?'

'No,' I had to admit, 'I can't be sure.'

'In that case,' Wystan was still smiling as he came to pronounce his verdict, 'you probably did little but alienate the judge and irritate the jury.'

I had nothing to say to that and, for a dreadful moment, I thought he might quite possibly be right. 'It's true, however,' Wystan fortified himself with sherry before making the admission, 'that your asking those questions gave you considerable influence over our client, young Simon Jerold.'

'I think it did.'

'Of course, he has no knowledge of the law or the tactful conduct of trials.'

'Thankfully not. He didn't seem to want to invent a story about his father attacking him later that night.'

'So it's up to you, Rumpole, to use this influence you have obtained, in whatever doubtful way, to help our client.' Wystan ignored my tactless reference to the story he'd asked Simon to invent.

'That's what I intend to do. Help our client.'

'I'm glad to hear it. Very glad indeed.' At this Wystan put down his glass, sat up straight and fixed me with his pale eyes. 'So now will you use that influence to benefit young Simon? On Monday morning before the judge sits, you will persuade him to see sense?'

'Sense?'

'Yes, Rumpole, common sense. Tell him to invite me back. To take over, Rumpole, the conduct of his defence.'

'You want me to tell him that?'

'And in spite of his outrageous behaviour, I'm prepared to forgive and forget. I have asked Albert to keep me free for the next couple of weeks.'

I looked into his eyes and was reminded, strangely enough, of the eyes of Simon. Both of them were calling desperately on my help. I was horribly aware that I could only help one or the other, and the choice was inevitable. I started by saying, 'I mean to get him off.'

'You, Rumpole? Alone and without a leader?'

'Yes. If that's what Simon wants.'

'What Simon wants!' Wystan's pained expression was turning to anger. 'And you honestly believe he's innocent?'

'What I believe is immaterial, you know that at least. It's not for me to make a judgement, it's up to the jury.' Here was I, an inexperienced white wig, telling my Head of Chambers the basic rules of a barrister's life. 'It's my job to put his case as well as possible. He says he didn't kill his father or "Tail-End" Charlie. I've got to show that it's at least possible that he didn't murder anyone.'

'Rumpole!' Wystan called me to order. 'You say

150

it's your job. I'm merely asking you to tell the client to agree that it's your leader's job. Will you do that on Monday morning?'

It seemed from a far way off that I heard myself answering, probably unwisely, 'No.'

'Did you say no?' Wystan couldn't believe his ears.

'No is what I said.'

'May I ask why you said no?'

'Because I've just had a long talk to Simon. Because he's got some hope at last. Because he seems to have come back to life and almost made a joke. I can't deprive him of all hope.'

'Are you suggesting, then,' Wystan for once asked a question like a good cross-examiner, 'that my presence in the case would deprive our client of hope?'

There was no answer to this, so I didn't give him one. He gave up persuading and passed to a judgement which, I suppose, I had made inevitable.

'Rumpole! Young men who join chambers with no practice and no previous experience are necessarily marked "on approval". We not only expect them to provide work for chambers but, perhaps more importantly, to live up to the finest traditions of the bar, by which our lives at Equity Court are, I am glad to say, governed. I have to admit that, at first, you showed promise. This was noticed by Albert Handyside, our clerk, and by my daughter, Hilda, who takes an interest in legal matters and who had some idea of pursuing a career at the bar, which proved to be impracticable.'

'Because of the toilet accommodation?' I was unwise enough to interrupt.

'For reasons of Chamber management which will no longer concern you, Rumpole! As I say, it was Hilda who persuaded me that you might be of some use as a very junior junior in *R.* v. *Jerold*. She is usually a sound judge of character and I took her advice. I very much regret I was unwise to do so. Disloyalty, Rumpole, is not in the finest traditions of the bar, and for a junior to turn the client against his leader is not conduct I can tolerate from a member of Equity Court. I advise you to start looking for alternative accommodation. You may have some difficulty finding it. Your reputation has already gone round the Temple, and Heads of Chambers have got little room for tenants who will seek to make fools of them in public.'

I can't say that this sentence was unexpected. There seemed to be little else to add, and there was no plea in mitigation which I could make without further wounding Wystan or betraying Simon. 'So, that's that, then' was my final speech as I stood up to go.

'Yes, Rumpole.' At last Hilda's daddy and I seemed to be in agreement. 'That would appear to be that.'

'There is one more thing.' That's the trouble with barristers, they always have something else to say. 'You asked me the one important question.'

'And what was that?'

'If Simon didn't kill his father and Charlie, who on earth did?'

'Oh, yes.' There appeared in C. H. Wystan's face something very like a sneer. 'And I suppose you've found the answer to it?'

'Not yet,' I told him, 'but I certainly mean to try.' And then we parted company.

To cheer myself up, and banish all memories of sherry, I cooked myself bacon and eggs with a fried slice on my gas ring and washed it down with the bottle of Château Thames Embankment I had bought from Pommeroy's one optimistic evening when Albert gave me a Legal Aid cheque.

I went to bed with Wystan's question echoing in my head. Who on earth else? I had no idea of the answer then, but only a feeling that somewhere, perhaps in my long talk to Simon, there lay the first hint of an answer. I could get no further than that, and then the sight of Daisy Sampson floated across my mind and I remembered the lost case of Uncle Cyril Timson. For a moment his story seemed to have some connection with the mysterious happenings at the Penge bungalows. But not being able to work out exactly what it was, I fell asleep.

17

Looking back down the long corridor of the years, as I have had to do in the writing of these memoirs, I have come to the conclusion that life is a game of chance, like roulette or beggar my neighbour, and not a game of skill, like chess. There seems to be no sense or logic in the cards we are dealt. For instance, why on earth did my fiancée, Ivy Porter (daughter of my old law tutor at Keble), who was young, I thought beautiful, cheerful, happy, full of jokes and doing no harm to anyone, have to die so young? There was no sense at all in this, while those human beings we could quite honestly do without (here I might mention the names of Their Honours Judge 'Custodial Cookson' and the mad Bullingham) soldier on until a ripe old age doing nothing but bring about injustice, frustration and irritation to those unfortunate enough to appear before them. By what ill chance was there a Luger pistol with a magazine full of bullets available in the Penge bungalow on the night when young Simon Jerold had a quarrel with his father?

But Simon's tragedy was, of course, my great opportunity, so whoever is dealing out the cards at random has no idea who will be the winners or losers. When I thought about this I felt ashamed, almost guilty. Did this young man have to risk his neck so that I could land a sensational case in the public eye? My shame at this thought had to be banished by a renewed determination to save Simon's life, if I could, if only I could! I thought of the chances that had brought me into this position, all of which I had accepted gratefully. If Daisy Sampson hadn't danced away from me I might not have, I told myself, so impressed Hilda by my walk around the floor that she recommended me for a junior brief in a case which her father had got, certainly more by luck than by good management. If he hadn't been called away to the Court of Appeal that morning, I wouldn't have been able to cross-examine the great forensic science oracle and inspire hope in Simon. And now here I was, landed with all this good fortune, with no real idea of what to do with it when we started work again on Monday morning.

I'd gone out to breakfast at a greasy spoon near Southampton Row and come back home with the hope of working out some sort of plan of attack, when the next card came fluttering down from the sky and it promised to be, if not an ace, at least a royalty. My landlady told me there'd been a phone call and she'd written down what was for me an unforgettable number. I put money into the pay telephone in the hall and was rewarded by the slightly breathless and ever welcome 'Hello, darling' of Bobby O'Keefe.

'You rang me! Are you going to leave that three-fingered husband and come down to join me for the weekend?'

'He's right here with me in the bar, Rumpole.'

'Is he jealous?'

'Not in the least. He wants to know if you're still grounded.'

I couldn't help a feeling of resentment at ex-Pilot Officer Dougherty's complete lack of jealousy, but I pulled myself together. 'Well, yes,' I said, 'I am grounded. Doing a big case with not an idea in my head.'

'Your ears would have been burning a couple of nights ago. There was a chap in here, taking a week's holiday in Coldsands with his new wife— very nice girl too. Anyway, he was interested in all the stuff we have over the bar and he told us he used to fly Bristols in the war, so naturally Sam and he got talking.'

'Naturally.'

'And we mentioned that case you're meant to be doing at the Old Bailey. We told him we knew you and he was interested in that too.'

'Did he say anything else apart from being interested?'

'He wanted to put you straight about a couple of things.'

'He knew Jerry Jerold?'

'He seems to have done.'

'All right. Did he say what he wanted to put me straight about?'

'Not really. He didn't say any more. Then he bought us a round of drinks and we got at the piano.'

'I wish I'd been there.'

'Well, you should stay down here. Not keep up in that London.'

'Did he have a name, this well-wisher?'

'He left us a card. He's a salesman in something. Home loans. Pensions. Patio paving. Something we don't want anyway.'

'The card, Bobby! Have you got the card?'

'I think Sam had it somewhere. Sam!' She called out across the bar, empty before opening time, and they started up a search. I waited in suspense until it was found, tucked in beside an upended bottle of

Haig and Haig behind the bar. His name was Don Charleston and his card disclosed a telephone number.

It was as a result of this, and a subsequent call, that I found myself on Saturday lunchtime walking past the maze, the lake with flamingos and various significant buildings, towards the end of the Crystal Palace Park.

'You'll find him,' Don Charleston's wife had told me on the telephone, 'by the prehistoric animals.'

What was that about? Was he in the company of a coven of circus judges or hugely outdated Conservative politicians? I asked her what she meant exactly.

'He's having access.' She pronounced the word as though it was an attack of an unfortunate illness like asthma or epilepsy. '*She* only gives it to him half a day a month. That's by order of the court. It hasn't made any difference since we got married. It's only half a day a month he can have Jimmy with him. And you know what's all that boy wants to do? Go to Crystal Palace Park and stare at the bloody dinosaurs, if you'll pardon my French. What did you say your name was, Mr . . .'

'Rumpole. Horace Rumpole.'

'Well, that's where you'll find them, Mr Rumpole, if you're all that interested.'

Crystal Palace Park, for those unfamiliar with the locality, was the place to which Joseph Paxton's great greenhouse, an enormous palace of glass, was moved from Hyde Park after the Great Exhibition of 1851. It burnt down before the Second World War, and what was left were fragments of buildings, lakes, a site for concerts, a motor-racing track and a football ground. And this strange collection of

158

lakes and buildings exists, of course, around Penge.

I had my instructions from Mrs Charleston, who, I imagined, derived her strength and much of her energy from constant criticism of the cruel and unnatural ways of her husband's first wife. The park was full, at the weekend, of lovers, mothers pushing prams, children running away from their parents, getting lost and called for down the walkways, and street sleepers with nothing better to do, turning their faces to what was to be almost the last of the September sun. Somewhere on my way I passed a bust of the poet Dante. 'Abandon all hope, you who enter here,' was what I was repeating to myself, and yet I was full of hope now that I was about to meet another possible player in the Penge Bungalow tragedy.

When I reached the prehistoric animals I saw them almost at once, a tall man with curly greying hair and a small boy, perhaps seven years old. They were sitting together on a bench with what was left of a picnic lunch on a neat cloth between them. The boy was staring at an island on the lake where a variety of stone dinosaurs were assembled. To look at them seemed pleasure enough for him; he didn't want to hear them bellow or see them flop into the water and paddle their way to the footpath.

'Mr Charleston?' I said.

'Who the hell are you?' The man looked up suspiciously, but his voice was quiet, with a strong Scottish accent.

'My name's Horace Rumpole. I'm a lawyer.'

'I've got the boy till three o'clock. I've got the right to be with Jimmy till three provided I don't bring him into contact with my present wife, Marjorie Charleston. I don't know what sort of lawyer you are, but you'll see that down in black and white in the court order.'

'No, no,' I did my best to reassure him. 'I'm a friend of Bobby Dougherty, O'Keefe that was. She said you were staying down at Coldsands.'

'Our only holiday. Working too hard all the summer to make what I have to pay to Jimmy's mother. Surely she doesn't begrudge us a week's holiday at the sea with a bit of rain attached to it.'

'I don't know what your ex-wife begrudges,' I assured him, 'I know absolutely nothing about her. As I told you, I'm a friend of Bobby and Sam Dougherty. Mind if I sit down?'

'If you have to.'

I was not getting the warmest of welcomes from the ex-air force hero as I squatted on the bench beside him. On the other side was the check tablecloth, folded in four, and on it was the refuse of rejected crusts of spam sandwiches, prepared, I imagined reluctantly, by the present Mrs Charleston, the end of a chunk of fruit cake and empty bottles of Tizer. Jimmy never turned to look at me during our conversation, having eyes only for the prehistoric monsters.

'I've got absolutely nothing to do with your divorce,' I assured Jimmy's father. 'I'm the lawyer who's defending young Simon Jerold in the Penge Bungalow case.'

'That's right!' Don Charleston seemed to be gently congratulating me on remembering at long last who I was. 'That's right! They were talking about you up at Coldsands.'

'With approval, I hope.'

'They seemed to like you. Bobby likes you at least.'

160

'She also said you were talking about the late Jerry Jerold.'

'He was a brave man, that's all I know about him.'

'Is it? One of his fellow officers, a chap called Harry Daniels, thought Jerry richly deserved what he got, which was shot through the heart. Do you agree?'

I waited for what seemed a long time for an answer. Don Charleston was occupied clearing up the remains of the picnic, putting the crusts of sandwiches and empty bottles into a carrier bag. He flapped the cloth in the air, scattering crumbs that were swooped on by the birds. When he sat down again he said, 'The boy's just fascinated with the monsters. He can't get enough of them.'

'They don't look particularly friendly.'

'They used to roam the earth. You should remember that about them. It was nothing but a swamp with those monsters roaming about. Nothing changes, does it, Mr Rumpole?'

I thought this was a rather too pessimistic view of our situation so I said nothing.

'They made those statues from fossils found in the British Museum. You knew that, I suppose?'

'I'm afraid I didn't.'

'That's the old pterodactyl Jimmy's looking at now.'

The monster did, I thought, have a legal look, with wings sprouting from legs like the folds of a gown and a long beak open to discuss fees or deliver judgements.

'So many of you living in the same part of south London.' I started some gentle probing. 'The address on your card was Norwood, and then there were Jerry and Charlie at Penge of course. And Peter Benson over at Sutton.'

'Now he's having a good look at the iguanodon.' Small legs supported the huge animal with a monstrous pointed tail and a hungry grin. 'That's meant to be the masterpiece, but they got it wrong,' Don told me. 'That sort of horn arrangement shouldn't be on its nose. It should be a kind of gigantic thumb.'

'That's all very interesting, but we were talking about Jerry Jerold. Did you keep in touch with him after the war?'

'From time to time, yes. And I want you to get this clear, Mr Rumpole, whatever you call yourself. Jerry never did anything wrong. He never did anything that would make him deserve shooting. He was a brave officer who crashed his plane and got taken prisoner. That's all Jerry was.'

'His son says that he turned against the war.'

'His son! After he shot his own father, he'd tell you anything, wouldn't he?'

'I'm not sure.'

'Well, you can be sure of one thing. It's no good you asking around to find bad things about Jerry. Because there aren't any.' Don took his son's hand and said, 'We'll have to get going soon, Jimmy.' The boy nodded, now gazing at the iguanodon as though it was about to waddle hugely towards us.

'Sam Dougherty told me how scared people were in bomber command.' I tried to keep the subject open.

'Scared? Of course we were scared!'

'What else can you tell me about Jerry?'

'Tell you? I can't tell you anything else. Peter Benson knew Jerry best. You'll have to ask him.'

162

Peter Benson, who had disarmed Simon and who spent evenings in the pub with Jerry. 'He got on well with Jerry, didn't he?'

'They were great friends. If you want to know more about Jerry, you'll have to ask him.'

'I'll have to do that in court,' I told him. 'But I've got a young man, a solicitor's clerk. His name's Bernard and I call him Bonny. Could he get a statement from you? You may be able to remember more about Jerry then.'

'I'm not going near any lawyers or any court of any sort. Not ever. Not after the battle we had over Jimmy. Why should I?'

I gave him what I thought was the inescapable reason. 'They want to hang young Simon. Suppose someone wanted to do that to your Jimmy when he was grown up? You'd do anything in the world to save him, wouldn't you? Just try and remember!'

'I don't know who you are, Mr Rumpole.' Don's voice was still gentle, but his meaning was perfectly clear. 'I've told you absolutely nothing. If you get me in court I'll say just that you must have made our conversation up. I told you, I'm not going near any court or answering questions from lawyers, not ever again as long as I live. Come on, Jimmy. I've got to take you back to *her*, and we don't want to be one minute late, do we?' He dismissed me with a brief, 'You'll excuse me, Mr Rumpole.'

I left him then, uncomfortably aware that I had been brought to a meeting that had told me nothing. The puzzle remained without a solution. The question of whoever had a reason to kill Jerry Jerold, apart from his son, remained unanswered. So why had Don Charleston troubled to leave his number with Bobby O'Keefe, and why was I led to

163

the park to learn about nothing but prehistoric animals? Was it, I wondered, a meeting arranged to tell me that there was nothing to tell? Even if that was the truth of the matter, it brought me no nearer to a defence for Simon.

Just before I left the park I turned back to look at the enigmatic Don. By then he was deep in conversation with a tall man in a long blue overcoat who had a pale face and a lock of black hair falling across his forehead.

18

To add to my troubles, Hilda's daddy had turfed me out of chambers, so I was going through my brief, checking my notes for cross-examination, in the Tastee Bite in Fleet Street. There I was at breakfast, satisfying myself on eggs on a fried slice, sausage, tomatoes and bacon, with some strong coffee, an intake of carbohydrates which was to see me through decades of difficult mornings down the Old Bailey in the times to come.

I had polished off the main part of this strengthening meal when I heard a sharp cry of 'Rumpole!' and Hilda, carrying a cup of coffee, came and plumped herself down beside me. 'I've been watching you, Rumpole. If you go on eating breakfasts like that, do you know what you're going to be, without doubt, in the future?'

'I hope a successful defender of those in trouble with the law. A man with a mantelpiece loaded with briefs.'

'No. You're going to be fat.'

'I'm going to fight for young Simon's life,' I told her. 'I need a certain amount of nourishment to do it properly. Whether I become fat in the process is a matter of no concern to me.'

'But it may be of some concern to your wife.'

'My wife? I have no wife in view at the moment.'

'Have you not?' She gave me the sort of patient smile of which I was to see more in the future. It was a smile that said, 'You have very little idea of what's going on at the moment and I really can't be bothered to explain, but you'll probably see sense in the end.' Then she said, 'I've been talking to Daddy.'

'Your daddy,' I was bold enough to tell her, 'turfed me out of chambers. It's because of your daddy that I have to prepare a day's work in the Tastee Bite eatery, or in the robing room at the Old Bailey. I am homeless as a result of your daddy.'

'Perhaps you shouldn't have taken over his case. He's not too pleased about that, Rumpole.'

'So he told me.'

'All the same I managed to have a word with him on the subject of you.'

'On the subject of me?'

'I told him you were doing a difficult case . . .'

'Didn't he know that already?'

'If you could stop talking for a moment, Rumpole, and just try to listen. I got him to agree you could go on using Uncle Tom's room while you're doing *R*. v. *Jerold*. Uncle Tom's hardly ever there.'

'I know. That was kind of you. Did Daddy take a lot of persuading?'

'He was against it at first.' And Hilda added with pride, 'I wore him down.'

'You did very well.' I had to admit Hilda at her best would have worn any court down and forced any judge or jury into submission. I was about to tell her how utterly mistaken her daddy was, both in his conduct of the trial and in denying her a seat in Chambers, when her voice rose in a tone of accusation and disapproval. I had my wallet open on the table beside me, preparatory to drawing out a ten-bob note towards the Tastee Bite's terms for breakfast. As I picked it up, the recent purchases

166

from my landlady's shop slipped from their moorings and three rubber johnnies, still regrettably in their packets, were exposed to the view of the future She Who Must Be Obeyed.

'Not before it's legal, Rumpole. We can't think of that sort of thing yet, can we? Only when it's legal, don't you agree?'

By now my thoughts were on the day in court ahead and I didn't feel I could spare time discussing the illegality of rubber johnnies.

'Oh, I suppose so,' I said, and, 'Sorry, I've got to pay the bill and get down the Old Bailey.'

As I left Hilda was smiling in a way that seemed almost triumphant. She had, after all, retrieved my room for me, at least for the duration of the trial, and so I smiled back.

*   *   *

I was walking down to Ludgate Circus on one of the last of the golden September mornings, with my brief in a very junior barrister's blue bag slung over my shoulder. All the facts it contained were, as usual, circulating in my head and still coming to no very coherent conclusion.

Outside the old Palais de Justice, flashes went off from a few cameras, because the newspapers now knew I was defending Simon alone and without a leader. I felt a moment of pride, which I knew immediately was no substitute for a decent defence, and dived in through the swing doors and took the lift up to the robing room.

There various barristers were getting wigs and gowns out of their lockers, standing in front of mirrors, fastening winged collars to their studs, tying on crisp white bands and doing their best to turn from a haphazard collection of odds and sods into a solid and uniformed body of learned friends. As I was tying the bands and adjusting the wig I heard, with my usual irritation, the Old Etonian bray of the prosecution junior.

'How are you today, Sherlock Rumpole? Getting ready to go down with all your guns blazing? Dressing up to sink beneath the waves?'

'Rumpole?' I heard the voice of a stranger who was tying on his bands close to Reggie Proudfoot. 'Isn't he the chap that's agin you in the Penge Bungalow Murders?'

'Of course he is. The boy in question fired his leader and so he's got Rumpole. Rumpole's a most useful defender if you want to get convicted. You've heard the story about Rumpole at London Sessions, haven't you?'

'I don't think so.' It was the voice of the stranger.

'Vincent Caraway told me. Rumpole was defending some old codger who was just longing to go to prison. Of course Rumpole obliged and got him two years.'

And then suddenly, as Reggie Proudfoot said that, an extraordinary thing happened. It was as if a hand had given a final shake to the kaleidoscope and a new pattern emerged; as though all the questions and statements and speculation of the last weeks had settled down into one, perhaps almost credible, explanation, and the connection between Uncle Cyril's defence and the deaths of Jerry Jerold and 'Tail-End' Charlie became clear. Now I had a lot more to think about, but first I had to express my gratitude.

'Thank you, Proudfoot!' I said, clasping the wig

to my head. 'I can't tell you how grateful I am to you for saying that!' And with that, I pulled my gown about me and left the abominable Proudfoot in a state of considerable surprise.

I took the lift down to Court Number One and there, in the usual crowd of people waiting for the entertainment to start again, I saw Bonny Bernard.

'You seem very cheerful this morning.' Young Bernard was not quite able to understand it.

'I feel,' I told him, 'like some watcher of the skies when a new planet swims into his ken.

'Or like stout Cortez, when with eagle eyes
He stared at the Pacific—and all his men
Look'd at each other with a wild surmise—
Silent, upon a peak in Darien.'

So, with a bit of Keats for company, I strode into court in an unexpected mood of hope.

19

'How is old Rumpole?'

'Very well, thank you.'

Dodo Mackintosh was chiefly remarkable for her small pointed nose, thick woolly cardigans and her habit of smiling broadly at any item of bad news. She lived near Lamorna Cove in Cornwall, where, so far as I could discover, she spent her time scrambling over the rocks and painting in watercolours. It was one of her works, which showed this beauty spot in what looked like a fine rain, that hung over our mantelpiece.

'You won't be well, will you, Rumpole,' She Who Must had to chip in with a discussion of my health, 'if you don't do what the doctor told you and keep your leg elevated.'

'Circulation?' Dodo asked with her head cocked on one side, a broad grin and a knowing look.

'Of course.' She Who Must nodded in serious agreement.

'If you don't keep that old leg of yours up, you may have to lose it, Rumpole.' The idea seemed to cause Dodo increased amusement. She fairly bubbled with laughter and I had to remember her help in preparing cheesy bits for chambers' parties before I could find her in any way tolerable.

'Rumpole is working on his memoirs,' Hilda explained. 'He says he can't keep his leg up and write at the same time.'

'That's ridiculous.' Dodo seemed to find the situation funnier than ever. 'Hundreds of people must have written their memoirs with their legs up.

What are your memoirs about anyway, Rumpole?'

'The Penge Bungalow Murders. You won't have heard of them.' I insured myself against the danger of another good laugh from Dodo and a denial that any such epoch-making case ever existed.

'She's heard you talk about it often enough,' said Hilda. 'Come along, Dodo. We've got to go shopping.'

'Shopping?' I was wary. 'Surely we've got everything we need.'

'Don't you remember? We've got all the girls coming for the after-theatre party.'

'Who's coming exactly?' Dodo was curious.

'Sandy Butterworth and—'

'Not Sandy Butterworth?'

'Yes. What's wrong with her?'

'She was the one who spread terrible rumours about Miss Bigsby and the school janitor.'

'Miss Bigsby the maths mistress?'

'Science and biology.'

'It wasn't Sandy that said that. It was Emma Glastonbury,' Hilda thought.

'No. I'm sure it was Sandy Butterworth.' Dodo stood her ground.

'Or was it one of the Gage twins? That janitor was rather handsome.'

'Dunc the hunk we called him. His name was Duncan.'

'Of course it was.'

So they went off, discussing the evidence in the case of Miss Bigsby and the janitor, and I pushed my chair nearer to the gas fire and contemplated my memoirs, in which the issues were far more serious than the question of who'd slandered Miss Bigsby.

I went into Court Number One at the Old Bailey, as I have reported, after a sudden enlightening feeling, as chuffed as stout Cortez when taking his first view of the Pacific. What had been said by Reggie Proudfoot in the robing room had suddenly thrown a bright light on what was, up until then, only a dark suspicion in the corner of the Rumpole mind. It seemed to be the simple answer to a simple question, but how I was to get it into the evidence, or what I could do with it if I got it there, remained a mystery as yet unsolved.

So when I got up to cross-examine an important witness, the hands were once again damp and the mouth dry. In a way the idea I had made the job more difficult. All I could do was to fire off as many questions as possible in the faint hope that one of them would startle a cowering covey of truths and send them flying out into the open. The witness in question had given his name as Martyn Dempsy and his occupation as curator of a small geology museum attached to a south London civic centre. He had studied the subject, he told the court with a good deal of pride, after he left the air force. He also declined to take the oath as he thought all swearing was an insult to God and Lord Jessup allowed him to affirm. All of this made him, I felt sure, a serious witness the jury would instinctively trust. He stood, a gaunt figure in the witness box, suddenly removed from the rocks and fossils of his small and rarely visited museum.

'Mr Dempsy,' I began in a tone which I hoped was friendly, 'you were in the same squadron as

173

Jerry Jerold and Charles Weston?'

'I was.'

'Did you get to know Jerry Jerold well?'

'Pretty well, yes.'

'Tell me this. Was there a time when he got, shall we say, pessimistic about the war?'

'He had his gloomy times, yes. Some of us did.'

'But did he take it further and say Hitler was bound to win?'

'I can remember him saying that once or twice,' the reliable witness agreed reluctantly.

'What did you say to him on those occasions?'

'I told him to stop talking like that and get on with the job.'

'Very commendable. And did he take your advice?'

'Until his plane was shot down. Yes, I believe he did.'

'Until his plane was shot down.' I repeated this for the benefit of the jury, and then asked, 'Did you see much of Jerry Jerold after the war?'

'Not very much. We met at a few reunion dinners, that sort of thing.'

'Was it a surprise when he asked you to this theatre party?'

'A bit of a surprise, yes. He asked a number of people from the squadron. We all paid our way.'

'And what was the purpose of this party, do you think?'

Here Winterbourne rumbled to his feet and objected that the witness couldn't possibly know what was in the deceased's mind. The judge, unfairly I thought, said, 'Yes, Mr Rumpole. You have only recently become familiar with the rules of evidence. Apply your knowledge to this case,

174

would you be so good?' After which, he snuffed a large helping off the back of his hand. I waited for this operation to be over, and when the silk handkerchief had been applied to the judge's nostrils I rephrased the question. 'Was there a discussion of your wartime experiences?'

'Not a general discussion, no.'

'Did you hear the deceased, Jerry Jerold, say anything about *his* wartime experiences that evening?'

Winterbourne rumbled another objection, but I was able to argue that, as Simon was accused of murdering his father during a quarrel about the war, the deceased's views on this subject should be relevant. The question was allowed.

'I heard Peter—'

'That's Peter Benson?'

'Yes. I heard them discussing prison.'

'We've heard from my learned friend in opening this case that Jerry Jerold was a prisoner of war.'

'Yes.'

'You know that he was?'

'Yes, of course. He talked about it often.'

'Often?'

'Whenever we talked about the war.'

'On the night of the murder was anything more said by Jerry Jerold about his wartime experiences?'

'Only when Peter Benson proposed a toast to the memory of David Galloway.'

'David Galloway being the navigator who died when the plane caught fire.'

'Yes.'

'Who proposed the toast?'

'Peter Benson. In the Cafe Royal, before we went to the Palladium. It was rather peculiar.'

'How peculiar?'

'Peter Benson proposed a toast to David's memory. Then he congratulated Jerry and Charlie Weston on their extraordinary luck in getting out of a burning plane without catching fire. He said it was a pity David didn't have their luck.'

'How did the party take that?'

'I would say with embarrassment.'

'And how did Jerold react?'

'He asked us to raise a glass to David, "a good friend and a brave officer". I think by that time Jerry had had a good deal to drink.'

'And did you raise a glass to David Galloway?'

'I do not touch alcohol.' As though to illustrate this, the witness took a great gulp of water from the glass provided.

'Mr Dempsy, if we could come to the night of the alleged murder—'

'I'm glad to hear that!' The judge's voice was as silky as his handkerchief. 'I have allowed you a good deal of latitude, Mr Rumpole. The jury may think that the evidence we have just heard has some connection with the quarrel about the war. On the other hand, they may not. They may feel that you have been wasting the court's time.'

'On the other hand, My Lord,' I was by now calm enough to reply, 'they may not. By the end of the case, they may have found it extremely helpful.'

The Lord Chief Justice's eyebrows shot up towards his wig. 'This is not the time, Mr Rumpole, for you to comment on the evidence one way or the other.'

'I'm sorry, My Lord. I thought as you were commenting—'

'Mr Rumpole!' The silk handkerchief had gone

176

from the judge's voice, which was now as soothing as a Brillo-pad. 'One of the lessons you apparently still have to learn is to be careful what you say in the presence of the jury.'

'Careful? If I ever became as careful as C. H. Wystan, you might as well fix the date of Simon's execution now. I have absolutely no desire to become what is known as a "safe pair of hands"!' I didn't, of course, say any of this, but I thought it as I moved to safer ground, the party in the bungalow. 'Mr Dempsy, when the party got back to the bungalow had all the others drunk a good deal?'

'They drank in the interval at the Palladium. And we stopped at a bar before we got the train, yes.'

'And when they got Simon out of bed, he poured out whisky.'

'That is so, yes.'

'But you saw all that was going on with a clear and sober eye?'

This got a few smiles from the jury but the geologist, sipping water again, remained serious.

'I can remember what was going on, yes.'

'What was going on was a father blaming his son for being too young to fight in the war.'

'You could put it like that.'

'I'm not suggesting you joined in, but some of the others did, didn't they?'

'Yes.'

'Was there a man called Harry Daniels there?'

'Yes. I knew him in the war.'

'Did he tell the others to leave the boy alone?'

'I think he did.'

'Have you seen Harry Daniels lately?'

'I'm afraid we've lost touch since the murder.'

177

'I understand. We've rather lost touch with him too.'

'Mr Rumpole!' The judge clearly showed his displeasure. 'If you want to give evidence, you should go into the witness box. Whether you could get in touch with this man Daniels is quite irrelevant.'

'If Your Lordship says so,' I gave him the retort humble, 'then of course I accept it. Mr Dempsy—' I turned back to the witness to indicate that, as far as I was concerned, the matter was closed—'let me take you to the moment when there was talk about killing.'

'"You're so keen on teaching people to kill people. I promise you I'll kill the first of you that touches me. So you'd better watch out."' The judge was reading from his notebook.

'Exactly.' I gave His Lordship a small bow and tried to keep any suspicion of irony out of my voice. 'I'm grateful to Your Lordship for reminding the witness.'

All I got there was a glare and the judge took out his irritation on the lid of his snuff box, to which he administered a severe tap.

'You heard him say that, Mr Dempsy?'

'Well, the boy—'

'Simon Jerold?'

'Yes. He picked up the gun and pointed it at his father.'

'Mr Dempsy, we know that there was a separate magazine that held the bullets. Did you see young Simon fit the magazine on to the gun?'

'No, I didn't see that.'

'Are you sure you didn't?'

'Yes.' The witness thought it over again. 'I'm

178

sure he didn't.'

'So you would agree with Mr Wardle, who gave evidence last week, that Simon was threatening his father with an empty gun?'

'I suppose he was, yes.'

I waited patiently for His Lordship to make the note I expected of him. After he had done that without too much of a show of reluctance, I allowed myself to turn to the jury with a look of moderate triumph. Up to this moment I was enjoying the cross-examination, but I was about to move into a dangerous area and ask questions when I didn't know the answers.

'The gun was taken from Simon by Peter Benson.'

'I saw that, yes.'

'Did young Simon Jerold put up any sort of struggle for the gun? Did Mr Benson have any difficulty taking it away from him?'

'Not so far as I could see, no.'

'Not so far as I could see.' The judge repeated the qualification while he made the note. Young white wig as I was, I wasn't having that. 'Were you looking at the couple as the gun was taken away?' was what I asked the witness.

'Yes, I was.'

'If there had been a struggle for the gun, would you have seen it?'

'Yes, I'm sure that I would.'

'Thank you very much, Mr Dempsy. Now, let me ask you this. After the gun had been removed from Simon, what happened to it?'

Dempsy frowned. 'I really couldn't say.'

'Was it put back on the mantelpiece, for instance?'

'I didn't see that, I'm sure.'

'What about the magazine? Did that stay on the mantelpiece?'

'I'm afraid I can't remember that. We saw Simon bang back into his room.'

'How long did the party go on after Simon left it?'

'Everyone stayed on for about an hour.'

'About an hour after the business with the gun?'

'Yes, that's right.'

'So doesn't that mean that no one took that young man's behaviour with the gun particularly seriously?'

'I don't think we did take it too seriously. At the time.'

I paused then to make sure the answer sank into the minds of the jury. Then I asked, 'Was it a happy party, after the gun incident?'

'Not really.'

'Will you tell the jury what you mean exactly?'

'Jerry Jerold was drinking quite a lot . . .'

'Ever since Peter Benson had proposed a toast to the navigator?'

'Yes, after that. Jerry seemed on edge. Excited at times. At others, well, he could be quite rude. He got at me for not drinking and then became, well, morose. Perhaps he felt guilty about the way he'd treated his son.'

'Perhaps?'

'Or perhaps I'm just imagining things.'

'No, Mr Dempsy, I don't think you are. When did you leave?'

'In fact I was almost the last to go.'

'Tell us about that.'

'I'd ordered a taxi because I knew I'd be late and

it was held up or something. Only Peter Benson, Jerry and Charlie were left. The atmosphere seemed worse. I can't explain why.'

'Just tell us what happened, if you would.'

'I'd been to the bathroom and I was washing my hands with the door open. The bungalow's quite small. You can hear what's going on in other rooms.'

'Tell us what you heard.'

'Well, I heard Peter Benson say something more about David Galloway.'

'Tell us.'

'Peter said, "He just wouldn't play ball with you, would he?" Then there was a bit I didn't hear, until I heard Peter say something about "surrender" and "execution".'

'Execution?' There was a sudden complete silence in Court Number One at the word, all of us, no doubt, thinking of the young man alone in the dock.

'That was what he said. Then someone called me, I think it was Charlie, to say my taxi had arrived.'

'And you never saw Jerry Jerold or Charles Weston again?'

'Never.'

I suppressed a whoop of joy, I even tried not to smile. Whichever god looks after white-wigged barristers out of their depth in an important criminal trial had just handed me an unexpected slice of luck. Martyn Dempsy the geologist had turned up trumps. I gathered my gown about me and sat down, giving the jury a look which meant, 'There you are. I told you so, and we'll hear a great deal more about that before the case is over.'

Meanwhile, Winterbourne had rumbled to his feet and sounded as though he thought it extremely bad form for one of his witnesses to give unexpected evidence apparently so satisfactory to the defence.

'Mr Dempsy,' he began to re-examine in a pained growl, 'you said nothing about what you heard from the . . .'

'Bathroom?' The witness helped him out.

'Yes, from the bathroom, in your statement to the police.'

'I wasn't asked about that.' Dempsy supplied the answer. 'They were only interested in the time young Simon Jerold picked up the gun. That's all they asked me about.'

'You say you heard some talk about the navigator, Galloway, and then you picked up the words "surrender" and "execution".'

'Yes. It was Peter Benson I heard say something like that.'

'Something like that? I shall be calling Peter Benson later in this trial and he may tell us about that conversation. But did it mean anything to you?'

'Not at the time, no.'

'I must confess it makes no sense to me either.' The judge was tapping his snuff box in a dismissive sort of way. 'Nor do I suppose that it makes sense to the jury. We can only hope that the time may come when Mr Rumpole will tell us what his defence to these serious charges is exactly.' At this he snuffed up a generous pinch of brown powder and said, 'Ten-thirty tomorrow morning, members of the jury,' and rose to his feet.

As I stood up and bowed, I told myself that the time when Mr Rumpole could disclose his defence had come considerably nearer.

*   *   *

The next morning we started on the evidence of other guests at the party, but I won't weary you, or give myself the trouble of going through all their testimony in these memoirs. It's enough to say that they agreed that Simon had given up the pistol without any trouble, that they couldn't remember seeing it put back on the mantelpiece and that the party continued for about an hour or more after this dramatic incident.

Another week had almost passed. Tom Winterbourne announced that on the following morning he would call his most important witness. He spoke as though it was his treat, saved up until the end of the meal on Friday afternoon. Accordingly, when we knocked off on Thursday, Bonny Bernard and I descended once more to the cells to get final instructions from our client.

I remembered, when I first saw Simon Jerold in prison and in prison clothes, he seemed like a disembodied spirit, a young man on his way to almost certain death, remote, incomprehensible, entirely different from us, his legal team, who, whatever verdict the jury came to, would be allowed to go on living.

He had been given his best suit for his days in court: a dark blue jacket and trousers suitable for going to church on Sundays, or starting work in a bank, getting married or facing a trial for double murder. At the start of the trial it seemed that the same disembodied spirit inhabited this formal suiting, which was a size too large for it. But when I went down to the cells after court that Thursday our client seemed to have signed a new lease on life. If he wasn't entirely cheerful, a smile lit up his face from time to time. He looked as though, like me, he was a young man who had just joined the defence team and was now convinced of the possibility of success.

'You got that Martyn Dempsy, Mr Rumpole. You really got him! He had to admit that he never took my threat with the gun seriously. Of course I'd never have shot anybody.'

'He didn't take it seriously at the time. When he read in the papers that your father had been shot in the night, I should think he took it very seriously indeed.' Luckily the rumbling Winterbourne didn't put that to Dempsy in re-examination. In fact I didn't say this to Simon, allowing him to feel a moment of optimism instead of plunging him back into a world of despair. I asked him to tell me a little more about Peter Benson, who'd be in the witness box the following afternoon.

'I always liked him.'

'You did?'

'He used to talk to me a lot, more than some of Dad's friends did when I saw them. They hardly seemed to notice my existence.'

'He took the gun away from you.'

'He did the right thing. I was stupid. I should never have picked it up. If I hadn't done that, I shouldn't be where I am today, should I?' He said this with a sort of surprise, as though he had just woken up to this simple fact from some confusing nightmare.

'So you liked him and he was one of your father's best friends?'

'He was,' Simon sounded doubtful, 'until they began to, well, not quarrel exactly, disagree.'

'When was that?'

'Oh, not too long ago. I'd say a few months before Dad got shot. Peter was talking a lot about David Galloway.'

'The navigator who died?'

'Yes.'

'What about him?'

'Well, he said Galloway's family had never been satisfied with the "missing, believed dead" story. And it seems one of them was in France lately, near the place where the plane came down, and he heard something, some old rumour from members of the Resistance, about an English flying officer who'd been found dead, shot near an abandoned plane.'

'Shot?'

'Dad told Peter that couldn't possibly have been David Galloway, because he died when the plane caught fire.'

'Did that finish the argument?'

'Not quite. Peter also said someone in the family thought he might have been a prisoner. Of course they never heard, but neither did we hear about Dad.'

'How did it end?'

'Well, for some reason Peter wanted to get the records of Dad being a prisoner, and he couldn't get them without Dad's consent.'

'So did Jerry give his consent?'

'No. I think he found it a bit of a cheek that Peter asked.'

'I'm not surprised. Were you there when they disagreed?'

'I heard some of it. Then I went into my bedroom.'

'And there was no one else around?'

'Only Joanie.'

'Joan Plumpton, the cleaning lady?'

'Yes. We shared her with Charlie. I know she was in and out cleaning. I don't suppose she understood what it was all about.'

'We can find out. They'll be calling her as a prosecution witness. Did Peter and your father say anything else you can remember?'

'Not really. Dad refused to let Peter look into the records, so they parted.'

'No longer friends?'

'I don't know. Dad often said he regretted not seeing Peter. I think the idea behind the night out at the Palladium was to show he still wanted to be friends. He was very pleased when Peter accepted the invitation.'

'Perhaps he was.' I thought this over and then I asked Simon a question which no doubt surprised him. 'Can you remember what Peter Benson was wearing when they came back to the bungalow?'

Simon closed his eyes as though that made it easier to remember. At last he said, 'His overcoat.'

'What sort of overcoat?'

'Long, dark, I think. I remember he kept it on after they got back. He said the bungalow was cold, which it wasn't at all.'

*   *   *

'You got any more jobs for me, Mr Rumpole? Nothing else to make enquiries about?'

'I don't think so. We're about as ready as we're ever likely to be.'

We had come up, Bonny Bernard and I, from the cells at the Old Bailey and in the entrance hall I saw Daisy Sampson in close conversation with Reginald Proudfoot, the prosecution junior. She peeled herself away from this particular pain and, as she approached me, she was full of congratulations. 'Well done, Rumpole! You were going great guns in there this afternoon.'

'You were there?'

'In the back of the court. I had an hour to kill, so I squeezed in.'

'To see your friend Reggie, the prosecution pain?'

'To see you both.'

'He doesn't perform much. His leader hasn't let him call a single witness.'

'And you're on your feet all the time, aren't you, Rumpole?'

'I'm alone and without a leader.'

'So I bet you've got some devastating stuff to throw at Reggie's star witness.'

'Who's that?'

'What's he called? Benson?'

'Peter Benson, yes. Do you know what I've got to throw at him? I mean, do you want to know?'

'If you want to tell me, Rumpole.' She gave me one of her most encouraging smiles. But I remembered our conversation in the Hibernian Hostelry. 'Or does Reggie Proudfoot want to know?' I asked her.

'To be absolutely honest, I've hardly discussed your case with Reggie at all.'

I had been long enough at the bar to know that the words 'to be absolutely honest' are usually followed by a thumping lie. I was starting to learn that the world can be a very wicked place, particularly the world of solicitors' clerks and junior barristers. 'Tell Reggie Proudfoot,' I instructed Daisy, 'that he'll just have to wait and see.'

*   *   *

'I thought they'd turfed you out of chambers.' Surprised by my entrance, Uncle Tom missed the wastepaper basket and his ball rolled away under what was again my desk.

'They have, but I'm allowed to use this room during the case. Thanks to my learned ex-leader's daughter.'

'They told me in the clerk's room that you were

doing quite well.'

'Not yet. We can't say that yet.'

'Odd they should turf you out of chambers because you're doing well.'

'I think that was why they did it.'

'Damned odd!' Uncle Tom thought it over and could come to no reasonable explanation. He retrieved his golf ball and left me to it.

I gave myself a small cigar. I had no need to go through the prosecution statements again as I knew them by heart. Half an hour later I heard the voice of C. H. Wystan saying goodnight to the clerk, Albert. He didn't call in to say goodnight to me. All I knew was that the day when I had to stand up and cross-examine Peter Benson would come inevitably, and when it did I would have to fire off all that remained of my ammunition. I put away my brief at last and went down to Pommeroy's and bought myself a solitary Château Thames Embankment. As I drank it down I wished myself luck.

Before I went to sleep I thought again of the strange connection I had been shocked into when Reggie Proudfoot called me a loser in the robing room. Was Jerry Jerold exactly like Uncle Cyril Timson in that they both thought that, in the different circumstances of their lives, prison was the safest place for them? This thought, which had made me feel as elated as stout Cortez when it first occurred to me, had survived the evidence of Martyn Dempsy and even been strengthened by it. Whether it would survive the evidence of Peter Benson, I was about to discover.

190

'Call Peter Benson. Call Peter Benson.'

The name echoed down the hall outside the court. I was checking my notes as he took the oath, and then I looked up and saw the tall, pale man with a lock of black hair I had first seen among the prehistoric monsters in conversation with my non-informant, Don Charleston.

When he had taken the oath, ex-Pilot Officer Benson answered Winterbourne's questions quietly but clearly and then looked round the court as though anxious to see the effect he was having on us all. I noticed that he looked everywhere but at the dock, where Simon was now watching him attentively. No doubt conscious of it being Friday afternoon, and knowing the lure of His Lordship's pigs in Berkshire, counsel for the prosecution took Benson quite quickly through his evidence so, sooner than I had expected, I was on my feet, ready to play any card left in my hand and hope for the best.

'Mr Benson, did you like Jerry Jerold?'

The question was unexpected and there was a long pause before the witness answered. 'We knew each other for a long time. We were in the same squadron. And we went on seeing each other after the war.' Then he was silent.

'You haven't answered my question. Perhaps I can help you. Do you remember when Jerry Jerold turned against the war?'

'I'm not sure what you mean.'

'Aren't you? Did he say that Hitler was bound

to win?'

Again the witness took a long time to answer. I was thinking of a perhaps over-elaborate plan concerning a man called Don Charleston who had wanted to find out why I went to Coldsands and whom I was told to meet in Crystal Palace Park. Was that meeting to persuade me that Jerry never said anything of the sort?

'We've all heard a prosecution witness say that Jerold was convinced Hitler was going to win. Are you suggesting that Mr Dempsy made that up? I shall be calling further evidence on the subject.' Faced with this threat of evidence, Peter Benson made his first concession, opening the door just wide enough for me to get my foot in it.

'He said something like that.'

'And did he say that we ought to make peace with Hitler and leave him to fight the Russians?'

'Some people thought that, yes.'

'And was one of them Jerry Jerold?'

'At one time, yes.'

'And was that about the time his plane is said to have crashed somewhere over France?'

'It was round about then. It was all a long time ago.'

'So I ask you again, did you like Jerry Jerold?'

'I didn't like what he said.'

'So you didn't like him for saying that?'

'I told you. It was a long time ago.'

'But you didn't agree with what he was telling you?'

'Certainly not.'

At this point, it seemed to me that we were going well. Peter Benson had clearly decided that there was no point in arguing about Jerold's attitude to

192

the war. He knew about Dempsy's evidence and luckily he didn't know what other evidence I had to call on the subject. It was lucky he didn't know that, because young Simon was my only witness.

But my pleasure in the result so far was not shared by His Lordship, who was looking meaningfully at the clock on the wall of the court. 'Mr Rumpole,' he said, 'need we waste time on events which occurred years before the night these crimes took place? As the witness has said so rightly, it was all a long time ago.'

'My Lord, Mr Winterbourne in opening his case told the jury that Jerry Jerold was a war hero. I'm entitled to put it to the witness that he was perhaps not as heroic as all that.'

'Whatever degree of heroism he attained, Mr Rumpole, he didn't deserve to be shot.'

I don't quite know what degree of heroism I had reached as a white wig, but I was astonished at my new-found courage when I heard myself say, 'That's a question I intend to discuss with the witness in due course. May I also remind Your Lordship that, in view of the fact that this crime arose from a discussion about the war, you ruled I could ask questions about earlier talk on the same subject.'

'I'm beginning to regret I did that.' The judge was looking at the clock again.

'That was Your Lordship's ruling.'

'Oh, very well, Mr Rumpole. You may learn in the fullness of time that the most effective cross-examinations are those that are kept brief.'

'We'd finish more quickly if you took another snort of snuff and let me get on with it.' I didn't of course say that, my heroism hadn't reached such a point of daring, and perhaps never would. I turned to another subject. 'You knew David Galloway, the navigator?'

'Very well indeed.'

'Was he a particular friend of yours?'

'Perhaps my closest friend.'

'Until he died in the burning plane?'

'Until he was killed, yes.'

I repeated his answer. 'Until he was killed. But to keep his memory alive, you proposed a toast in the bar of the Cafe Royal.'

'I did that, yes.'

'May I remind you of the words you used on that occasion. They are in Martyn Dempsy's evidence, My Lord.'

The judge, who had been flipping back his notebook pages at high speed, said, 'Yes, I've got it, Mr Rumpole,' in a voice which meant, 'For God's sake, speed it up.'

'Did you congratulate Jerry Jerold and Charles Weston on their extraordinary good luck in escaping from a burning aeroplane without getting burned?'

'I may have said something like that.'

'Martyn Dempsy swore that you said exactly that.'

'Perhaps I didn't mean it entirely seriously.'

'It was a strange subject to joke about, wasn't it?' I waited for an answer and didn't get one, so I took an enormous and necessary risk. 'You never took the whole story of their plane crash entirely seriously, did you?'

'I don't know what you mean.' The witness tried a shake of the head and a tolerant smile.

The judge did his best to help by saying, 'I too

would welcome it if Mr Rumpole clarified the question.'

'Certainly, My Lord. This was the situation. Both Jerry Jerold and Charles Weston had become increasingly terrified of flying on their bombing raids, hadn't they?'

'Of course. We were all terrified from time to time. We weren't all on the ground staff like you, Mr Rumpole.' Benson got a small laugh for this and a warning from the judge that the witness was there to answer questions and not to discuss Mr Rumpole's war record, however humble it might have been. And I was left with the certainty that Benson had found out more about me than a witness needs to know.

'I can quite understand a bomber pilot's terror,' I assured him, 'and it must have reached a high level with those two pilots. But we have to add the fact that Jerry Jerold thought we would lose the war and no doubt persuaded "Tail-End" Charles to share his opinions.' It was then that the memory of Uncle Cyril Timson came into use. 'So they decided that prison was the only safe place for them. Is that what you suspected?'

'Do you mean an English prison, Mr Rumpole?' In the silence that followed my question the judge asked for further particulars.

'No, My Lord, a German prison.' And then I turned to the witness. 'Or perhaps something better than that, if they brought down the plane and handed it over to the enemy? Did you know that was their plan?'

There was another long silence, in which the jury were suddenly still and all staring at Peter Benson with increased interest. It took him a long time to answer, and when he did so it was hardly a denial. 'How was I to know what they planned? All we heard was that the plane was lost and they were, all three of them, missing. That was all we heard.'

'Until after the war?'

'Until Jerry came back to England, yes.'

'And did he tell you that David the navigator was caught in a burning plane?'

'He told us all that.'

'Did you believe him?'

'That was what he told us.'

'And were you deeply suspicious of the whole story?'

'Why would I be suspicious?'

'Because Galloway's family had heard something about an officer found shot near an abandoned plane. Did you tell Jerry Jerold that?'

'I may have done.'

'Did you?'

'Yes,' Peter Benson, who had no idea what evidence I was about to call, thought it best to admit it.

'So you started to check up on the whole story, didn't you? You wanted Jerry Jerold to agree to you getting confirmation that he'd been a prisoner of war.'

'He didn't want me to do it.'

'I know he didn't. So there was a quarrel?'

'A bit of an argument. Yes.'

'An argument because by then you couldn't believe Jerold's story?'

'There were things about it that puzzled me perhaps, yes.'

My foot had got further into the door, so I pushed it and dared to ask, 'Did it occur to you that

David Galloway might have been killed because he wouldn't agree to the surrender?'

'Which surrender are you talking about?' I got a dusty answer.

'The surrender of Jerold and Weston, those two officers.'

'How would I get an idea like that?' Peter Benson smiled.

'Over the years perhaps. When you had your suspicions and kept close to Jerry Jerold because you wanted to find out the truth.'

'And how do you think I'd do that?' Benson was cross-examining me.

'I'm not sure,' I had to confess. 'Perhaps from things Jerry said when you were out drinking together. Perhaps from your researches, when you couldn't find any evidence of his being an official prisoner of war. Did you imagine they might have got a warmer welcome from the enemy?'

'What the witness imagined,' the judge told me, 'is scarcely evidence. You can only ask him what he knew.'

'Very well, My Lord. Mr Benson, you knew a great deal and suspected more, didn't you, when you went on that night out at the London Palladium?'

Peter Benson's bright eyes flickered as he took in the whole court, again with the exception of the dock. Finally he was looking at counsel for the prosecution as though for help, but the growling Winterbourne had his head down, close to his notebook, and even Reggie Proudfoot failed to return his gaze, so no help was forthcoming from either of them. Again, he thought perhaps that a complete denial might be dangerous in the light of unknown evidence to come. He decided on a moderate concession.

'I thought there were questions still to be answered, yes.'

'Questions still to be answered.' I gave the jury a look to remember and said, 'So now we have reached the events in Jerry Jerold's Penge bungalow after the theatre.'

'I'm sure we're all extremely grateful for that, Mr Rumpole,' the Lord Chief Justice said with what I took to be a distinct note of irony and gave another look at the clock.

'You kept your overcoat on?' I asked the witness.

'I don't know what you mean.'

'Your overcoat. You kept it on until you left, and you were the last to leave.'

'I feel the cold. I haven't been well lately.' Again he looked round the court as though asking for sympathy. 'Anyway I thought I wouldn't stay all that long.'

'But things got dramatic and you did stay.'

'Yes.'

'What did you think of Jerold and some of the others baiting young Simon for not having taken part in a war?'

'I . . . I didn't like it.'

'Did you protest as Harry Daniels did and ask them to stop?'

'No. But I didn't join in.'

'Very brave of you! With your unanswered questions about Jerry Jerold's crashed plane and his admitted terror of bombing raids, didn't you think it was a bit rich that he attacked his son for not fighting in a war?'

'I may have thought that.'

'But you didn't say so.'

'No.'

I looked at the jury. I could see in their faces that they no longer felt any affection for Mr Peter Benson.

'We've heard that someone threatened to remove Simon's trousers and he picked up the Luger pistol.'

'And threatened to kill his father with it,' Peter Benson was pleased to add.

'And you were the one who got him to give up the gun.'

'I was.'

'No one else tried to do it?'

'I suppose I was the quickest.'

'Did he resist you? Did he try to keep hold of the gun?'

'Not very effectively.'

'The witnesses all say he let go of the gun without any resistance at all.'

'Let's say I was stronger than him.'

'And they all say they didn't see him put the magazine in. Did you see that?'

'I can't remember him using the magazine.'

'So we can agree that he may have been pointing an empty gun?'

'Perhaps he was at that time. Things may have been different later.'

'Oh, yes, they were. Entirely different.' I picked up a sheet of paper then, part of my brief, anything that would do to make the witness feel that I had more to back up my interpretation of the events of that night than an inspired guess and a curious faith in Simon's innocence. 'Every witness called by the prosecution has said that they couldn't remember you putting the gun back on the mantelpiece after Simon had gone to his room.'

'They may not have noticed.'

'Or you may not have put it back?'

'Of course I put it back.'

'Nobody saw you do it, Mr Benson. And do you know why nobody saw you?'

'I can't answer for them.'

'Because it went straight into your overcoat pocket. Together with the magazine, which you collected when the drinks began to flow again and nobody was looking.'

'That is entirely untrue!'

'Entirely untrue,' the judge repeated as he made his note and underlined the words.

'Why ever would I want to take the gun away with me?' The witness smiled at the jury, perhaps hoping to get them to join him in ridiculing the suggestion, but I felt I had at least held their attention.

'Let me try to help you. Here were two officers you thought apparently surrendering their plane and themselves to the enemy. What would have been the penalty if that sort of conduct had been discovered during the war? The penalty for treason.'

'I suppose . . . possibly death.'

' "Execution" was the word Mr Dempsy heard you use. And you had another score to settle with those two men, because you were sure they'd killed your friend David Galloway.'

'I told you, they said David died when the plane caught fire.'

'Of course they did—and you didn't believe them. So you saw your perfect opportunity to

200

do justice.'

'I don't know what you mean.'

'Let me help you again. Young Simon had threatened his father with a gun. In a shooting, of course he'd be the number-one suspect, and that's why he's sitting there in that dock, on trial for his life.' Here I pointed to Simon, but the witness wouldn't turn his face to look. 'So you could return later, perhaps an hour later, and execute both of the officers.'

'You mean murder.' The witness's quiet voice had sunk almost to a whisper.

'Yes, Mr Benson. That's exactly what I mean. And when you'd done it, all you had left to do was to wipe the gun and the magazine free of fingerprints and leave them in the Jerolds' dustbin as further evidence against the young man who may have to pay with his life for the crimes you committed.'

'That's not true! None of that's true.' His voice was almost dying when he gulped water and told the jury, 'Lies! From start to finish. Stupid lies.'

By then I had sat down, my best cards played. I had nothing left in my hand but Simon's evidence, and my final speech. I looked at the jury and managed to find, I told myself, the beginnings of doubt on some of their faces.

Meanwhile, the judge, whose interest in the time was still obvious, said, 'I have been looking at the clock. I expect you may have a number of questions to ask in re-examination, Mr Winterbourne?'

'Oh, I have, My Lord.' The prosecutor rumbled to his feet to help the judge's release.

'Then I suggest we adjourn now as it's Friday. Would Mr Benson be available to deal with your questions on Monday morning?'

'My Lord, indeed he would.'

'He's not of course to discuss his evidence over the adjournment.'

'My Lord, I'm sure he understands that.'

'Mr Rumpole, in view of the serious charges you've made against this witness and the pressure put on him, do you agree to the course I have suggested?'

I knew that whatever I said wouldn't make the slightest difference to His Lordship's decision. So Mr Rumpole agreed, with unexpected results.

22

'Luci Gribble tells me you're writing your memoirs, Rumpole.'

'That's true. And I've just reached the point of crisis in perhaps the most important case I ever did. Although, and I have to add this in all fairness, I have done many important cases, and even managed to give a feeling of importance to the dull ones.'

'But you are writing your memoirs in a room in chambers.'

'My wife, Hilda, has got an old schoolfriend to stay. My flat in the Gloucester Road is filled with loud laughter and hilarious accounts of life in the dorm and on the hockey field. I came here in search of quiet, Ballard. I have just reached a vital moment in my life, so if you'll forgive me . . .'

'You're dealing with your life in these chambers in this book, are you, Rumpole?'

'My legal life, yes.'

'During a great part of which I have been your Head of Chambers.'

'You are now.' I had to acknowledge it.

'And as your Head, I shall of course wish to see the chapters you have written about me before you have any thought of publication. Can I do that? I shall have to be satisfied that you have written nothing libellous and that I haven't been treated with ridicule and contempt. I know how greatly you are tempted to ridicule, Rumpole, even Her Majesty's judges.'

'Particularly Her Majesty's judges. At least some

of them.'

'So let me see.' Soapy Sam Ballard held his hand out, as though expecting to receive a bundle of manuscript pages.

'It absolutely can't be done.'

'Why ever not?'

'Because there aren't any chapters about you.'

'None?' Soapy Sam apparently couldn't believe it.

'Not a single chapter. And only a passing reference.'

'A *passing* reference?' He sounded deeply disappointed. 'What sort of reference is that?'

'A passing one.'

Ballard thought this over and then pronounced judgement. 'As your Head of Chambers and a leading counsel,' he pronounced his verdict, 'I feel I'm entitled to more than a *passing* reference in any account of your life in the law, Rumpole.'

'I'm sorry,' I told him—the man was taking up valuable memoir time—'I feel I've rather exhausted the subject.'

There was a pained silence then and Ballard said, in tones that were quiet and clearly intended to be menacing, 'This room is set aside for you to do your legal work in, Rumpole. To note up briefs and write opinions. I don't believe your tenancy covers the writing of memoirs. It's a matter I shall consider asking Luci Gribble to put on the agenda for the next chambers meeting.'

With which dire threat Soapy Sam withdrew, and I bit the end of my pen as I remembered those faraway days at the Old Bailey and took out another sheet of paper.

It was the longest weekend I've ever lived through. The hours seemed to take days to pass and the days felt like months. On Sunday morning my landlady, Mrs Ruben, unexpectedly brought up my breakfast, the full English on a tray, together with the copy of the 'News of the Screws'. '"Did you shoot pilot heroes?" Penge Bungalow barrister accuses' and there was my name, staring out at me and staring out at a nation eating a late Sunday breakfast and enjoying other people's tragedies. And then I thought of the number of deaths it had taken to get Mrs Ruben to bring me breakfast in bed and fell into a mood of bleak despair, considering that next week's newspaper would announce the verdict and terrible sentence passed on Simon Jerold.

The flicker of fame that Sunday morning had brought me was no doubt the reason for Teddy Singleton ringing me up and suggesting we might have lunch in the French pub in Soho and then, 'What about doing a movie?' I was grateful to him, as I had been for his handing over to me the brief in the Timson case. I was also thankful for anything that might take my mind off Simon and his troubles over some part of that long, empty Sunday.

Teddy had given up his velvet-collared overcoat and rolled umbrella when we met at the French pub, in fact called the York Minster, just off Old Compton Street. The walls of its small bar were crammed with photographs of artists and writers. At least, that's what Teddy Singleton assured me they were. The drinkers in the pub looked dazed, hung-over and not yet fully awake as they reached eagerly for their life-saving first whisky. Teddy,

205

dressed for Sunday in a tweed jacket and grey flannel trousers, shod with polished brown brogues, said, '*La vie de Bohème*. That's what you get a taste of in this French pub. Gaston!' He called to an elderly man with a luxurious moustache behind the bar. '*Deux* of your *vin ordinaire* for me and my learned friend, *s'il vous plaît*.' After a number of calls for '*encore du vin ordinaire*' from Teddy, we climbed the stairs to an almost empty dining room, where a pair of elderly and sullen waiters managed to ignore our existence for a considerable time, until Teddy eventually persuaded them to bring us '*deux* steaks, medium rare, with *beaucoup de pommes frites*'.

'Wystan's really going to kick you out of chambers, isn't he?'

'Do you think so?'

'Oh, I'm sure so. I mean, as I read it in the "News of the Screws", you're really doing quite well. Wystan won't be able to forgive you for that. He'll chuck you out with the empty sherry bottles.'

'You think he'd do that?'

'Of course. I say, you're not in any danger of winning that case, are you?'

'Sometimes I think I've got a chance. Most of the time I don't.'

'For God's sake,' Teddy was sawing away at the medium rare, 'if your chap gets off, Wystan'll have you out in the next ten minutes. He couldn't bear that.'

'If I get him off, it would be worth it.'

'You really think so?' Teddy seemed to find this hard to believe.

'Of course I do.'

'Then when you're kicked out, which you will be

whatever happens, let's you and I start a fun chambers.'

'What's a "fun chambers"?'

'Well, we could get some rooms just outside the Temple. Have them decorated by some really fun people. You know, one wall yellow and one blue sort of idea. And we can do fun cases.'

'What's your idea of "fun" cases exactly?' I was curious to know.

'Divorce is the most tremendous fun.'

'Really?' I felt I'd need a great deal of convincing.

'Who's up who and who pays,' Teddy told me, I thought mysteriously.

'What's that mean?'

'Well, it's all about sex. And people throwing their dinner plates at each other, and screwing money out of their husbands for adopting unusual sexual positions. It's generally about the fun ways married people find to torment each other.'

'I've done some of that in the magistrates' court,' I told him. 'I think I'd rather stick to ordinary decent crime.'

'Oh, well.' Teddy continued to smile cheerfully at the prospect of so much fun divorce. 'You'll probably change your mind when you're out on the street and homeless. Now, eat up, we're off to the flicks.'

That afternoon, Teddy Singleton and I sat in a darkened Odeon watching *Quo Vadis*. The emperor Nero lolled about, ordering various bloodstained events which took place in the Colosseum, a venue almost as fatal as the Penge bungalows. When we emerged blinking in the late afternoon, Teddy said, 'I'll find you a home,

207

Rumpole, don't worry your not so pretty little head about it.' Then he kissed me lightly on the cheek and wandered back into the purlieus of Soho.

I spent a mainly sleepless night, worrying about Simon and realizing that there was at least this to be said about fun divorce cases: very few of them ended in a sentence of death.

Inevitably the morning came and I was back in the Old Bailey robing room, where I was accosted by an unusually quiet and far less triumphant Reggie Proudfoot.

'Oh, there you are at last, Rumpole,' he said, as though I'd been deliberately hiding from him. 'My leader wants to see you as a matter of urgency. He's in the bar mess.'

'I'll go up right away.'

'You do that, Rumpole.' Reggie spoke with all the bitterness of a man who hadn't been invited to join the party.

23

It's notable that so many of the important events of
this period of my life took place, not only in court,
but while people were eating meals. When I got up
to the bar mess, on the top floor of the Old Bailey,
Tom Winterbourne was finishing up his breakfast,
wiping the last stains of fried eggs off his plate with
a piece of bread. His wig was off his head and was
nestling beside the toast rack. 'Sit down, young
Rumpole,' he said, 'and have a cup of coffee.'

I agreed to both propositions and then he
surprised me by saying, 'You know, your cross-
examination of Benson was so effective that the
witness in question has gone absent without leave.'

'What do you mean?' Could this possibly be
good news on a Monday morning?

'Moved on. Taken himself off and left no
forwarding address.'

'I suppose you'll find him.' I hurried to dampen
what might be a flickering but misleading light of
hope.

'I'm not so sure. The police have been round to
his flat, of course. It's all locked up and empty. The
neighbours said they saw him leave on Friday night
in a taxi. He had a case with him and no one's seen
him since. Of course, we didn't keep a check on the
ports and Northolt during the weekend. He may
have gone to ground anywhere in Europe.'

Gone to ground. Done the vanishing trick. The
disappearing act. It seemed to have happened to so
many people. Harry Daniels, who might have given
evidence helpful to the defence, had been

persuaded to go AWOL by somebody. The story started when Jerry Jerold and 'Tail-End' Charlie decided to disappear at a difficult moment of the war and now Peter Benson, star prosecution witness, had also melted away into the great unknown.

Tom Winterbourne pulled a piece of toast from behind his wig and started to butter it lavishly. 'Would you ever consider doing a bit of prosecuting?'

'No.' I didn't have too much difficulty in answering the question.

'Why not?'

'I suppose I'd rather get people out of trouble than into it, by whatever I might do in court.'

'That's very odd.' Winterbourne applied a thick coating of marmalade. 'I much prefer getting people into trouble. In fact I greatly enjoy it! All the thoroughly bad men and women in the world! I consider it's my mission in life to make them squirm.'

'And do you think of young Simon Jerold as one of the bad people of the world?'

'That remains to be seen.' He chewed his toast thoughtfully. 'We'll have to see what the jury make of it.'

So I wasn't going to do fun divorce cases and I wasn't going to prosecute. I was stuck with a life of crime. But it was the most anxious moment of one of the most alarming cases I was ever going to do. A matter, quite simply, of life and death.

We went back to Court Number One and further facts emerged, one of them being that Peter Benson had removed a large amount of money from his bank in cash on the day before he gave

210

evidence, as though he was already considering the possibility of flight before he entered the witness box. Mr Winterbourne asked for another adjournment for further enquiries.

Mr Rumpole said it was intolerable for Simon Jerold to be kept waiting for his fate to be decided merely because a prosecution witness could no longer face the court. He also wanted the jury to be told about Peter Benson cashing in a large amount of money.

Rather to my surprise, the judge agreed with Mr Rumpole on both points. The trial would start again the next morning and, if Mr Benson didn't turn up to be re-examined, we would have to make the best of it and go on without him.

After another day of waiting and nerve-racking suspense, Tom Winterbourne announced that the police were no nearer finding Peter Benson, and there seemed a strong likelihood of his having gone abroad over the weekend. He called his last witness, Joan ('everyone calls me Joanie') Plumpton, who acted as cleaning lady for both of the murdered men. She took the oath and, unlike the vanished Benson, looked straight at the dock and gave Simon a broad smile, which he returned faintly but, I thought, with gratitude.

Joanie told us that she had been working as a dresser at the old Streatham Empire, but now just did cleaning round the bungalows. She gave her horrified account of finding 'Tail-End' Charlie dead in his hallway when she opened his front door with the key she was allowed to keep. He lived alone in his bungalow and he was alone when she found him.

When I rose to cross-examine her Joanie gave

211

me one of her smiles and was clearly anxious to help. She remembered vaguely being in Jerry Jerold's bungalow when he was having an argument with one of his friends about his having been a prisoner of war. She thought things were going to turn nasty, so she went off to clean the bath. So the prosecution case ended on a note that was only just favourable to the defence.

It's often wiser for customers accused of crime to stay silent and sit in the safety of the dock, where they can't be cross-examined, rather than come into the dangerous witness box, where their evidence can be attacked and torn to pieces. As much of my case depended on Simon's account of his father's fears, I had no choice but to expose him as a witness.

So he stood in his best suit and, at first, the jury were reluctant to look at this young man, this boy almost, they might feel bound to condemn to death. But as time went on, and as his answers sounded modest, quietly spoken and reasonably convincing, some of the jury members turned to look at him, and their looks were not entirely unfriendly.

All Simon had to say is contained in my account of the meetings with him in the interview room under the Old Bailey, so I needn't repeat his story here. It's enough to say that he admitted he had been extremely foolish when he pointed the gun at his father, but he had never loaded it and, of course, never meant to shoot. Finally I asked, 'If it were suggested to you that your father attacked you later on that night and you shot him in self-defence, what would you say?'

'I'd say that was nonsense. He never attacked me

and I never shot him. I couldn't have done that and I never did.'

'And Charles Weston?'

'I never shot him either.'

Tom Winterbourne, of course, made the most of the fact that Simon never called the police or a doctor as soon as he saw his father bloodstained in the chair. Again Simon said he was worried he'd be blamed for his father's death, and he went for a walk to calm his nerves. If our case was no better after Simon left the witness box, at least it was no worse. I scribbled a quick note of reassurance and gave it to Bonny Bernard to deliver to the dock.

*   *   *

'Two men, two officers in the Royal Air Force, decide that the war is no longer for them. They have become terrified of their nightly raids, risking death, which they feel must come to them in time, over enemy territory—fighting a war they are sure is lost and in which they can no longer believe. Can you not understand, members of the jury, how anything, even a prisoner-of-war camp, seemed safer than that? So they planned to surrender. Was it prearranged with someone working for the enemy, or did they just think it would be enough to come out of the plane with their hands in the air? Whatever the plan, it's clear, isn't it, that David Galloway didn't agree with it, so he had to die. The story that he was the only one of the three to be caught in a burning plane may seem as implausible to you as it did to Peter Benson. So Peter Benson believed that both Jerold and Weston were traitors, who might well have been responsible for the death

213

of his friend. In wartime they would have been executed as traitors. In these days of peace, did he decide to become their executioner? That night presented him with a remarkable opportunity. It offered him a gun and a magazine. More than that, it offered him young Simon Jerold, whom everyone had heard threatening to kill his father. The execution of Jerry Jerold and "Tail-End" Charlie would certainly be blamed on Simon. So he talked about execution after the young man had gone to bed. You'll remember the witness Dempsy, who heard him. And so he returned later that night and shot both the men as they opened their doors to him. Shot them through the heart as they stood in their hallways, in the way the medical evidence and the positions of the bloodstains have been made clear to you.'

I had, of course, got to know the jury well during our days in court together. There was one red-faced, grey-haired man who smiled at the faintest approach to a joke, and I felt sure he was on my side. And there was a hawk-nosed, tweezer-lipped woman who never smiled whom I took to be the leader of the opposition. My task was to convert Tweezer Lips and strengthen Red Face with persuasive arguments to use in the jury room.

'Members of the jury, I don't have to prove my case against Peter Benson. He has chosen to run away and hide from this court, and that fact may persuade you that he has something serious to hide. The question you have to ask yourselves is that, given all this evidence, including the fact that he was the last person to be seen with the gun, is it possible that he committed the Penge Bungalow Murders? If you, as we would say you must, come

214

to the conclusion that he is very possibly the murderer, then you can't be sure of Simon Jerold's guilt and it will be your duty, and I'm sure your pleasure, to return a verdict of "not guilty".'

None too soon, I reached the peroration. 'In a day or two this case will be over. It's taken up just over two weeks of your lives. Soon you'll go back to your jobs and you won't have to think any more about the Penge bungalows and the Luger pistol, the magazine and the bloodstains in the hall. This case is only a small part of your lives. But for that young man sitting there in the dock—' here I swung round and pointed at Simon—'it's the whole of his life that's at stake. And I put that young life with confidence in your hands.'

So I sat down and felt, as I have since in so many cases, an extraordinary feeling of relief, as though some unbearably heavy load had been lifted from my shoulders. I had done all I could for Simon and my job was over. Now it was for the jury to decide. The Penge Bungalow Murders case was out of my control entirely. It was with a curious sense of detachment that I listened to the judge's summing up.

*   *   *

'Mr Rumpole,' he told the jury, and by then my name came quite easily to him, 'has provided little evidence of Benson's guilt. However, you are entitled to take into account the fact that he fled from that witness box and has, apparently, gone into hiding. That may or may not be a manifestation of guilt, it's for you to decide. You can take into account all the other matters that

215

emerged from the prosecution witnesses, the fact that Benson quarrelled with the deceased Jerold, his use of the word "execution" and so on. Mr Rumpole is right in telling you that if you think there is a real possibility that Benson shot them, you can't be sure of Simon Jerold's guilt. Remember, members of the jury, our law has always held that it's a greater horror for an innocent man to be convicted than that someone who may be guilty goes free.'

He took snuff then, but I felt I could have run up to the bench and hugged him, or at least shaken the hand which had carried the brown powder to the judicial nose. I, of course, restrained myself, and the jury were sent out looking, some of them at least, as though they were worrying about what the word 'manifestation' might mean.

*   *   *

'Have I got a chance, Mr Rumpole? That's all I want to know.'

'Of course you've got a chance. The judge's summing up was very fair. Quite favourable to us in fact.'

'Is it a real chance? Tell me the truth.'

'I'm telling you the truth. It's a real chance.'

The self-possessed Simon we had seen in the witness box had gone, disappeared completely, and he had drifted back to the Simon we first met, a creature already halfway out of this world, with his eyes full of terror. My detachment had gone and, although there was nothing more I could do, I felt the full weight of responsibility again. I saw nothing ahead but the impossible task of saying goodbye to him after a guilty verdict.

'Do *you* think I've got a chance?' Simon had turned, in his despair, to Bonny Bernard.

'You've got a good chance. Mr Rumpole's given you the best chance possible.'

'Is it the truth? You're not just saying that?'

'No, Simon, it's the truth.'

'I can't believe you.' And young Simon Jerold closed his eyes, as though not daring to look at the events to come.

After we left him Bonny Bernard and I sat in the canteen, our stomachs awash with coffee and our fears growing. The jury had been out nearly three hours, a long time in those days, and then, as now, a prolonged retirement was not good news for the defence. Bernard told me that his principal, Barnsley Gough, would be coming down. We tried to discuss the case, or other cases we might perhaps do together. And then such topics dried up and we sat in silence until, at very long last, the message came, the jury was coming back to Court Number One with a verdict.

The courtroom was gradually filling with the principal players in our two-and-a-bit-week drama. Simon was brought up from the cells and sat between the dock officers, staring at his hands as though afraid to look up. Hilda smiled down at me from the public gallery and raised her thumbs as a sign of encouragement, and then an extraordinary thing happened: Hilda's daddy, C. H. Wystan, wigged and gowned as though he had been fighting the case, slid into the seat in front of me just as the jury came clattering back into their places. The clerk of the court rose to ask the final question. Hope drained away from me like cold bathwater and I was sure the answer would be fatal.

'Will your foreman please stand?'

Neither Red Face nor Tweezer Lips rose to their feet. Instead an unremarkable sandy-haired man in the front row stood up.

'Have you reached a verdict on which you are all agreed?'

'We have, My Lord.'

'And do you find Simon Jerold guilty or not guilty of wilful murder?'

'Not guilty, My Lord.'

Of course I couldn't believe it at first; neither could Simon, who was looking round the court in amazement. The press benches emptied as the reporters ran out to queue for the telephones. And then, to my further amazement, C. H. Wystan rose in front of me and addressed the judge. 'May my client be released, My Lord?' He spoke with great authority, as though he'd pulled off a remarkable triumph.

'Certainly, Mr Wystan. It's good to see you back. Release the prisoner.'

'I'm much obliged, My Lord.'

The judge had spoken, and my part in the Penge Bungalow trial was over.

24

It was, I suppose, one of the best days in a long life when Simon Jerold, free and innocent, came out of the entrance of the Old Bailey, blinking in the light of the last autumn sun and the flashing of many press photographers. He was accompanied and closely attended by his one-time leading counsel, C. H. Wystan, QC. They were closely followed by our instructing solicitor, Barnsley Gough, whose moustached lips were stuck in a triumphant grin. Bringing up the rear of this procession came the foot soldiers, who had stood in the front line of the battle, myself and Bonny Bernard.

We stopped on the pavement outside the old Palais de Justice and Simon turned to me, holding out his hand, and I took it. He seemed dazed, as anyone might be who, having been sent down to hell, is suddenly told to clear off to the world above and get on with his life.

'How can I thank . . .' he began, with no clear idea of how to end the sentence.

'No need,' I told him. 'Absolutely no need at all. It's enough satisfaction that you've won the case.'

As the palms of our hands, now dry, were joined, the cameras flashed in my direction. They were accompanied by a word of warning from C. H. Wystan.

'Allowing yourself to be photographed for the daily press, Rumpole, is not in the finest traditions of our great profession.'

'You weren't exactly camera-shy, were you, my absent leader?' was what I didn't say.

While this was going on, a happily smiling Joanie had emerged from the court and, taking Simon's arm, steered him towards the taxi Barnsley Gough had hired on the Legal Aid to take Simon back to the lonely bungalow and out of my life.

There was the loud roar of a powerful motorbike as Tom Winterbourne sped past us, no doubt in pursuit of the thoroughly bad men and women in the world.

'Well done, Rumpole. Well done, indeed!' It was Hilda Wystan, down from the public gallery and apparently in a mood of euphoria. 'Are you walking back to chambers? I know Daddy wants a serious word with you.'

'He's already had one. About not getting my photograph in the paper.'

'Oh, much more serious than that! I'll have to go back to my boring secretarial course this afternoon. But not for long, I hope and pray. Certainly not for long. Tell you what, I'll walk you up to the Temple.'

So Hilda and I walked from Ludgate Circus, the route I had taken after our breakfast in the Tastee Bite with such feelings of pessimism and dread. Now I was bursting with pride, prepared to sink a whole bottle of Château Thames Embankment in Pommeroy's and perform a ritual dance of triumph on the lawns of the Temple gardens, with all the astonished members of the bar, white and dirty-grey wigs, leaning out of their open windows to applaud me. A serious talk with Hilda's daddy in his room in chambers seemed a poor sort of celebration.

'Don't worry about it.' Hilda was clearly doing her best to cheer me up when we parted. 'It's just one of those formalities we have to go through.

220

Daddy's not going to eat you, Rumpole.'

I never thought he was. It was Hilda's use of the word 'we' that I found a little confusing. Hilda clearly hadn't been invited to the summit meeting in her father's room. She peeled off at the entrance to Equity Court with a wave and wished me luck.

As I went into the door of Equity Court chambers Teddy Singleton, swinging his rolled umbrella and wearing his velvet-collared overcoat, came out. 'Are you up for a little chat with the old Wistful?' he asked me. 'Ready to start a "fun chambers" outside the Temple area?' and then went off laughing, having bestowed no kiss upon me. As I went down the passage, Albert Handyside emerged from the clerk's room, closed the door behind him and offered me, again no kiss, but more well-meaning advice.

'That was a good win, Mr Rumpole. A truly remarkable win. My sincere advice as a clerk with some thirty years, man and boy, of clerking in the Temple is to play it down, Mr Rumpole. Try not to refer to it in conversation. Don't smirk about it. Do your level best not to boast.'

'Do you really mean that?' I have to confess I was disappointed. 'I had been looking forward to a good many years of boasting about the part I played in the Penge Bungalow Murders.'

'You pulled off a good win, Mr Rumpole. Solicitors don't always like men at the bar who pull off a good win.'

'You mean solicitors like to lose cases? I must confess the idea hadn't occurred to me.'

'They've usually advised their clients that the case presents various difficulties and they can't hold out much hope. They don't like to be taken by surprise.'

'I think Simon Jerold was quite pleased to be taken by surprise.'

'He's a client. Clients are different. But my advice to you, sir,' it was the first time my clerk had called me 'sir' and it made me feel as though I had grown up at last, but his next piece of advice put me back in the junior league, 'when you see Mr Wystan now, I would advise you not to exaggerate the part you played in *R.* v. *Jerold.*'

'Exaggerate!' I have to say that by now Albert Handyside, for all his long experience of the law, was starting to irritate me. 'Can you exaggerate the part played by Hamlet, Prince of Denmark? He's not just a spear carrier, after all, is he?'

'I don't think,' Albert looked at me as though I were still a white wig who had much to learn, 'that you'll find that Mr Wystan has any great interest in Hamlet, Prince of Denmark.'

On this point, I was to discover, Albert had got it absolutely right. But my interview with C. H. Wystan took a course which came, I have to confess, as a complete surprise to me.

*   *   *

'Sit you down, Rumpole. I must say, you were a considerable help on *R.* v. *Jerold.*'

'You mean, I was a considerable help to Simon? You might even say I saved his life.' Wystan's greeting had been curiously friendly, but I was still convinced he was going to announce my eviction from the sacred precincts of Equity Court.

'I mean,' Hilda's daddy was leaning back comfortably in his chair, his fingertips pressed together as though as an aid to deep thought, 'you were not only a help to the client, Rumpole. You were a considerable help to me. As you know, I had other commitments which prevented me from leading you, as I wished to do, for the greater part of the trial.'

' "Other commitments", was it? I thought you were sacked for useless inactivity quite early in the proceedings,' was what I didn't say. I was astonished at the way my ex-leader could rewrite history. What I actually said was, 'Oh, of course, other commitments,' hoping at least that my tone of voice would make it clear that no commitment could be more important than a young man on trial for his life.

'That is the general impression around the Temple,' he assured me, and although I thought the general impression around the Temple must be pretty silly, I didn't say so.

'That having been said,' Wystan's fingertips were still pressed together so his hands resembled a church roof, 'you managed to produce a successful result.'

'Let's say I was lucky.' I remembered Albert's advice and my ex-leader looked suitably grateful.

'Luck of course played the greater part in it. Apart from that, I have to say that your cross-examination of the chief prosecution witness invited criticism. To accuse a witness of murder on what seemed to be pretty slender evidence is not, Rumpole, in the finest traditions of the bar.'

'Perhaps not.'

'You were lucky that the Lord Chief allowed it.'

'Extremely lucky,' I had to admit.

'It's not the sort of thing a leading barrister

would do.'

'Bloody lucky there wasn't a leading barrister around, then,' was what I didn't say. Instead I pointed out that my questions had caused Peter Benson to do a runner.

'Do a runner? Really, Rumpole, your language has been infected by the criminal practice you seem determined to pursue.'

As 'doing a runner' was clearly unacceptable, I gave Wystan a truncated quotation from *The Tempest* which seemed to stop the man dead in his tracks:

'He melted into air, into thin air . . .
And, like this insubstantial pageant faded,
Left not a rack behind.'

'Well, yes. I suppose so.' Wystan coughed and turned with relief to another topic. 'There is something else we have to discuss.'

'I know.' I wasn't prepared to argue. Perhaps a 'fun chambers' with Teddy Singleton would be a good idea. 'I know I've got to leave Uncle Tom's room as the case is over. I should be able to find somewhere now.'

'No, it's not that.' He sounded impatient. 'It's not that at all. I've just had a long conversation with Hilda.'

'Hilda?'

'My daughter, Hilda. Of course, I've known all about it for a long time.'

'All about what exactly?'

'What was going on.' He was growing impatient, as though I was being unusually dense. 'It seems that you two reached an agreement when Hilda

224

joined you for breakfast at a café in Fleet Street.'

'The Tastee Bite?'

'Is it? I don't know the name.'

The famous breakfast eatery was only about fifty yards from the entrance of Equity Court, but C. H. Wystan had never dropped in for a couple of eggs and a fried slice. But what was the exact significance of my encounter with Hilda there? I asked for further and better particulars. 'You say we reached an agreement?'

'Well, you know what happened better than I do, Rumpole. You agreed that any sort of . . .' Here he searched for a word and at last settled for, '*familiarity* between you should be postponed until you were legally married. That was a correct and proper decision, and of course I commend you for it. I'm afraid it's not always so with young couples nowadays.'

'Married? Did you say married?'

'Well, of course. What else could you have been discussing?'

'Nothing. No, of course not, absolutely nothing.' How extraordinary it was, I thought, that the purchase of three rubber johnnies before dinner with Daisy Sampson should have such far-reaching results.

'My daughter, Hilda,' C. H. Wystan was summing up the situation, 'is strong-minded and usually persuasive. You may well find, Rumpole, in what I hope will turn out to be a happy future for both of you, that when Hilda has made up her mind to such and such a thing, it usually happens.'

'I imagine,' I told him, 'that might be so.'

'It is so, Rumpole. So Hilda has persuaded me that you should remain with us here, at Equity

225

Court, as a member of the family!'

'If I could have a little time to think about it . . .' I began, but our Head of Chambers was against any form of adjournment.

'I'm sure you've thought about it, Rumpole, long and hard. And now, dear boy, to celebrate our entirely new relationship, what about a glass of sherry?'

My heart sank as he approached the dusty decanter in the corner cupboard. This again was an offer I felt I could not decently refuse.

25

'Daddy agreed, Rumpole. I talked him into it!'

We were in the Temple gardens. Hilda had come in to me as soon as I had repossessed Uncle Tom's room and suggested we go into the gardens, where no one would overhear us and start talking. The leaves were gently turning to gold and the chrysanthemums were still out and the roses starting to fade. I wasn't whooping or doing a wild triumphal dance and the windows of the surrounding chambers remained shut. But I was still euphoric after winning the case alone and without a leader, as I shall always claim, in spite of C. H. Wystan's attempts to get in on the act.

We enjoyed a period of silence and then I said, 'Your father seems to be discussing marriage.' It sounded stupid as I said it. I would have to have been deaf and blind not to understand what C. H. Wystan was talking about.

'You've got it, Rumpole!' Hilda was laughing as though my slowness in the uptake was nothing but a joke.

'My marriage to you?' I ventured.

'Well, I don't know who else would want to marry you. I shouldn't think that Daisy Sampson's particularly keen on it, is she?'

'No, I don't think she's particularly keen.'

'Then you did well to propose to me.'

She was in the jolliest of moods, with a broad grin, shining eyes and a voice full of enthusiasm. I didn't want to spoil the moment for her, but I felt I had to ask her to remind me, 'When did I

227

propose exactly?'

'When we were having breakfast. Don't you remember? And you told me we shouldn't use those things until we were married.'

'I said that?' I was still puzzled.

'I think winning *R. v. Jerold* has been too much for you.' Hilda looked at me judicially. 'I think the excitement has blotted out bits of your memory. *Of course* you said that. Anyway, I understood exactly what you meant when you said it.'

'Did you, Hilda?'

'And I gave it a lot of serious thought. Of course I realized you're young and inexperienced and you could probably be quite irritating. But then I remembered all the time and trouble I'd invested in you.'

'Time and trouble?'

'Of course. Who got the junior brief for you in *R. v. Jerold*? Who cheered you up from the public gallery? Who praised your talent for cross-examination? And who told Daddy to keep you in chambers because I knew I could make something of you? Daddy said you were now one of the family. He wasn't wrong, was he, Rumpole?'

I was still in a high mood after Simon's acquittal and I felt the world was open to me. Hilda was quite right, she had supported me all along and she was unaccountably anxious to spend her life with Rumpole. There seemed to be no particular reason why a brave new world shouldn't have a marriage in it.

'Well, Rumpole?' The young Hilda looked as if, at that moment, she was about to have a fit of the giggles. 'I ask you again. What've you got to say for yourself?'

'There is a tide in the affairs of men,' I told her, 'which, taken at the flood, leads on to fortune. Omitted, all the voyage of their life is bound in shallows and in miseries.'

'Oh, for heaven's sake, Rumpole! Talk sense! Don't just show me you know your Keats.'

'It's not Keats. It's *Julius Caesar.*'

'Well, whatever it is, tell me what you think?'

'I think we might as well get married,' was what I didn't say. 'Well, yes, Hilda. Of course.'

'Oh, Rumpole! I'm sure I can make something of you.'

And with that, she threw her arms around me and gave me the sort of approving but not yet sensual kiss of those, at that time, who were now officially engaged.

*   *   *

'Now we come to number six on the agenda.' Luci Gribble, the person responsible for our chambers' image and administration, read it out at another chambers meeting. 'The question of the use of chambers rooms to deal with accessing accommodation in the workplace outwith its legitimate usage for targeting a successful, money-wise profession at the bar.'

'Perhaps you'd like to speak to that, Rumpole?' Soapy Sam Ballard was once again in charge of the meeting, during which Luci Gribble frequently referred to him as 'Chair'. Indeed, he had all the charisma and sense of fun of an article of furniture.

'What do you want me to say to it, Ballard? Except for the fact that it's a complete insult to the tongue that Shakespeare spake.'

'That item was put on the agenda because it came to my attention that you were using your room in chambers, and the heating and light provided—'

'Not to mention the coffee,' Claude butted in, unnecessarily I thought.

'Not to mention the coffee provided, very reasonably at cost. Thank you, Erskine-Brown. You were using the room, Rumpole, for a private purpose, completely unconnected with your practice at the bar.'

'What on earth do you mean by a private purpose? I haven't been using my room for a strip show, or devil worship or calling up the spirits of long-dead barristers. I've been writing an important chapter of legal history. You're only annoyed because you thought I hadn't written about you. I told you there was a reference to you.'

'You said a *passing* reference, Rumpole.'

'That was what annoyed you, wasn't it? Well, let me tell you, I compared you to none other than the famous C. H. Wystan, our Head of Chambers in the days gone by.'

'You compared me to him?' Ballard seemed somewhat mollified.

'He was also my father-in-law during the course of his long and not unhappy life. His conduct at the bar put me in the way of my greatest success.'

'You mean you learned from him, Rumpole?'

'Several important lessons.'

'And you've learned from me, I hope.'

'As my Head of Chambers, you are almost exactly like C. H. Wystan.'

'And you made that clear in your writing?'

'Crystal clear. Anyway, my memoirs are

230

now completed.'

'In that case,' Sam Ballard gave me a particularly soapy smile, 'I think we might pass on to item number seven on the agenda.'

'Pass on to it,' I gave him permission, 'and let the world know exactly what happened at the Penge bungalows on that extraordinary and fatal night.'

*   *   *

After the chambers meeting, Erskine-Brown came up to me in the corridor to apologize. 'Was it a bit mean of me to mention about the coffee?'

'You have a mean streak, Erskine-Brown,' was what I felt I had to tell him.

'I'm sorry, Rumpole. I'm not quite myself today. Lala Ingolsby spoke to me.'

'Amazing!' I agreed. 'What did she have to say?'

'That she's marrying a fellow called Gunnersbury who practises in the Chancery Division.'

'Cheer up. They're not all bad in the Chancery Division.'

'No, but it was the sad way she said it, Rumpole, and the sad look she gave me. No doubt at all she had still hoped we could somehow get together. But it couldn't be, Rumpole. It could never, ever be!'

So he mooned off and I went back to the mansion flat in the Gloucester Road, knowing it would be empty because it was the night when Hilda and her schoolfriends had planned their visit to the theatre.

*   *   *

It was almost eleven o'clock, just as I was contemplating sleep, when they came back and filled the kitchen. Dodo Mackintosh transferred her talent for preparing cheesy bits to scrambled eggs and I opened bottles from my private store of Château Thames Embankment. Once again the conversation turned to the question of who had been guilty of starting the rumours about Miss Bigsby, the mistress in charge of science and biology, and the school janitor, known as 'Dunc the hunk'.

'I'm sure it was Hilda who spread that story around.' One of the Gage twins made the accusation and I challenged her, on Hilda's behalf, to prove the charge beyond reasonable doubt.

'Rumpole has finished his memoirs,' Hilda told them by way of causing a diversion.

'I have,' I assured them. 'The world can now learn the truth about the Penge Bungalow Murders.'

'Learn the truth?' I think it was Sandy Butterworth who asked the question.

'Who knows?' I wondered. 'After any trial, who knows what the whole truth was exactly. All I know is that I won it. Alone and without a leader.'

'And did it make you famous?' This from Dodo Mackintosh.

'Not really. I sat in chambers and didn't get another brief for about a month. And then it was one of the Timsons receiving stolen fish.'

'You should have gone into commercial law, Rumpole.' Hilda shook her head sadly. 'Turned your talents to big companies suing each other. I could have made something of you if you'd been a

232

commercial barrister.'

'I'm sorry.' I had to confess that I'd devoted myself to a life of crime and was now beyond redemption. Then I filled a glass and lifted it. 'I would like to propose a toast,' I raised my voice against the gossip from the schooldays, 'to the person who supported me during the Penge Bungalow trial, who encouraged me from the public gallery and who stopped her learned daddy from kicking me out of my room in chambers. So, will you all charge your glasses and drink to She Who Must.'

'To whom?' My wife looked puzzled.

'To you, Hilda.'

'I thought you might want to drink to that dreadful Daisy Sampson.'

'Don't you remember? She married Reggie Proudfoot. No, I was drinking to you, Hilda. Entirely to you.'